450

THE WONDERFUL
WORLD OF CATS

THE WONDERFUL
WORLD OF CATS

Compiled by BETH BROWN

Pictures by LEONARD SHORTALL

HARPER & ROW, PUBLISHERS

NEW YORK AND EVANSTON

THE WONDERFUL WORLD OF CATS

Grateful acknowledgment is made to the following for permission to reprint selections included in this book:

"The Talking Cat" from *The Talking Cat* by Natalie Savage Carlson; copyright 1952 by Natalie Savage Carlson; by permission of Harper & Brothers.

"The Boy Who Drew Cats" from *Japanese Fairy Tales* by Lafcadio Hearn; copyright © 1953 by Liveright Publishing Corporation; by permission of Liveright Publishing Corporation and Nishinomiya & Hasegawa, Inc.

"Cats for Kansas" from *Cats for Kansas* by Le Grand Henderson; copyright © 1948 by Le Grand Henderson; by permission of Abingdon Press.

"King Solomon's Cat" from *Cat Tales* by Natalia M. Belting; copyright © 1959 by Natalia M. Belting; by permission of Holt, Rinehart and Winston, Inc.

"The Story of Serapina" from *The Story of Serapina* by Anne H. White; copyright 1951 by Anne H. White; by permission of The Viking Press, Inc.

"The Cat with the Crooked Tail" from *Wonder Tales of Dogs and Cats* by Frances Carpenter; copyright © 1955 by Frances Huntington; by permission of Doubleday & Company, Inc.

"The Cat Who Went to Heaven" from *The Cat Who Went to Heaven* by Elizabeth Coatsworth, copyright © 1958 by The Macmillan Company; by permission of The Macmillan Company.

"How Cats Came to Purr" from *The Pigtail of Ah Lee Ben Loo* by John Bennett; copyright 1928, 1956 by Longmans, Green and Company, Inc.; by permission of Longmans, Green and Company, Inc.

"Hey, Diddle, Diddle, the Cat" from *Up Hill Down Dale* by Eden Phillpotts; by permission of The Hutchinson Publishing Group.

"Benjamin West and His Cat Grimalkin" from *Benjamin West and His Cat Grimalkin* by Marguerite Henry and Wesley Dennis; copyright © 1947 by The Bobbs-Merrill Company, Inc.; by special permission of the publisher.

"Why the Cat Stares at the Moon" from *Animal Tales from Ireland* by M. Grant Cormack; copyright © 1954 by M. Grant Cormack; by permission of The John Day Company, Inc.

"The Cat Who Became Head Forester" from *Old Peter's Russian Tales* by Arthur Ransome; copyright 1917; by permission of Thomas Nelson & Sons, Ltd., Edinburgh.

"The Cat That Walked by Himself" from *Just So Stories* by Rudyard Kipling; by permission of Mrs. George Bambridge, Macmillan & Co., Ltd., The Macmillan Company of Canada, and Doubleday & Company, Inc.

"The Cat and the Mouse" from *English Fairy Tales* by Joseph Jacobs; by permission of G. P. Putnam's Sons.

"The White Cat" from *The White Cat* by Mme. La Comtesse D'Aulnoy, arranged by Rachel Field; copyright 1928 by The Macmillan Company; by permission of The Macmillan Company.

Grateful acknowledgment for their dedicated aid and encouragement—

to MISS SWEET, my first librarian in that childhood long ago, whose story hours fashioned me into a storyteller.

and to all the librarians since, including
MISS MARIA CIMINO, MISS MARIGRACE WELSH,
MISS ENDUN RAHMAN of the New York Public
Library, MRS. DOROTHY COLLIGNON BURTON of the
Montrose Library, Montrose, New York,
MR. NICHOLAS N. SMITH,
MISS MILDRED T. GRAULICH, LILLIAN G. CHAPMAN,
EDNA CORCORAN, MARTHA OWEN,
MRS. SYLVIA SALTZMAN of the Field Library,
Peekskill, New York, MISS PATRICIA FOLDY,
Frank G. Lindsey School, Montrose, New York,
ANNE IZARD, Childrens Consultant, Westchester
Library System, JULIA LOSINSKI, Young Readers
Consultant, Westchester Library System,
MRS. MARION E. DUNBAR, Union Catalog Librarian,
MISS KATHARINE M. HOLDEN, Director, Westchester
Library System, MISS FLORENCE WOLFINGER, Shrub
Oaks, New York, MRS. STELLA SCHLOSSBERG, Brooklyn, New York, MRS. CHARLES RESNICK, Lynbrook,
Long Island, New York.

My thanks to each and every one of you!

Contents

THE WONDERFUL
WORLD OF CATS

Calico, the Cat Who Earned Her Keep

by Beth Brown

IT WAS BETTY who saw Calico first.

Her mother and her father were standing on the porch with Mr. Benson, the real-estate man, when, suddenly, the doorknob turned and the front door opened as if by magic.

Everyone looked up expectantly to see who might be coming out of the empty house. The door closed. Then the doorknob turned again and the door opened again.

This time there was someone on the threshold. An old calico cat poised her lithe body for the briefest of instants, took in the strangers standing below with the briefest of glances, then came padding out on the porch. She settled herself on the top step and remained there, regarding the new arrivals out of intent green eyes.

"Now what do you call that?" asked Mrs. Warren.

1

"That's a cat," said Mr. Benson. He went on to explain. "It's Calico. Miss Osborn brought her here when she bought the house. They lived here together till Miss Osborn died. Seems like the cat won't leave the place. Miss Osborn loved that cat of hers—"

"Well, I don't love cats," snapped Mrs. Warren. "We're getting a dog for Betty."

Betty studied Calico. Calico studied Betty. An invisible bond of magic, like a bridge over which each could walk to the other, bringing them together, was suddenly flung through space. The girl and the cat raced across to meet each other and stood there, side by side, determined to go on together and not be parted by grownups.

"I don't want a dog," said Betty. "I want that cat."

"Be nice if you would keep it," added Mr. Benson brightly. "It sort of goes with the house, you know. Been here a long, long time. Smart, too. Did you see how it opened the door—all by itself?"

"I thought it was a ghost," remarked Mr. Warren darkly.

"My husband is right, Mr. Benson. That cat would remind me of Miss Osborn. The big house has echoes enough as it is." Mrs. Warren shivered. "If you don't mind, I don't want to live with the past. We're getting a dog for Betty."

"I don't want a dog," repeated Betty. "I want that cat."

"Look here, my dear," said Mrs. Warren impatiently. "We're not going to keep the cat. No, dear. Calico, or whatever is its name, has got to go!" She turned to the real-estate man. "I like the old house. It's nice and it's roomy. We'll take it, won't we, Mr. Warren?"

"Well," said Mr. Warren reluctantly, "it needs a lot of work. The gutters are gone. The porch is rotting and the bathroom is none too modern—"

"We've got a good plumber in this town," said Mr. Benson. "The best. I'll send him around in the morning."

"What about the cat?"

"We've got a good dogcatcher in this town," said Mr. Benson. "The best. I'll send him around in the morning."

The cat blinked at the words. She seemed to understand what was being said. An odd expression came over her face. Her green eyes filled with a green light. She turned the light on Betty.

"Oh, Mother!" Betty was pleading. "How can you? How can you send for the dogcatcher? She's such a beautiful cat. Just look at her, Mother!"

The cat blinked her eyes again, this time for Mrs. Warren.

The eyes were a beautiful, mysterious green and her coat was a beautiful brown and black with almost purple shadings, and her walk was graceful and her tail was long, a beautiful length. She was a beautiful cat, and smart besides. Smart enough to open a door all by herself and to stand there politely, listening to people without interrupting while they talked about ways and means of ending her life.

A cat like that, reflected Betty, should be asked to stay instead, coaxed with the choicest of tidbits not to seek another home. Why, Calico was really the nicest

thing about this new place that her father was buying. She looked at the old house with its dormer windows and its lacy wood trim, its wide porches and its generous gardens. A swing could go up into that big elm tree. A miniature lake could be made out of that shallow brown pond. A dollhouse could sit in the shade of those filbert bushes. But, best of all, a cat could share the sun of summer days with her and wait for her in the wintertime to come home from school and have a romp together.

But now her mother said there could be no cat, not even Calico, who had lived here long before them and practically owned the house.

How could she make her mother change her mind? How? How? How?

Three days went by without any sign of the dog-catcher. But he was sure to come. Mr. Benson had said so. This fact did not seem to worry Calico. Somehow the cat knew that she had a charmed life.

But Betty did not share her optimism. She knew her mother better than Calico did. Even though Betty was an only child, she did not always get what she wanted. Besides, her mother never changed her mind. She had said she had no use for that cat and the matter had been settled.

In fact, even feeding Calico posed a problem for Betty. Every night, when dinner was served, she would save something from her dish and hide it in her napkin. When she found the kitchen empty, she would sort out all the scraps, put them on a dish and bring them upstairs to her room. The dish would go under the bed.

At nine o'clock sharp—as if Calico had an alarm clock inside of her—while Betty was lying in bed, the door-knob would turn very slowly. The door would open very slowly. And Calico would come in very slowly. She never made a rush for the dish. First she greeted Betty with a smile and then she would stand there, waiting for Betty's greeting in turn.

"Hello, Calico," Betty would say.

Calico would purr softly like a lady. Then she would go to her dish, nibble her food, not gobble it, wash her face, dry her paws, purr good night and go out the door.

Betty loved their time together. She hated to think of the dogcatcher.

But early one morning, the telephone rang.

"It's Joe Higgins," said the voice at the other end.

"Yes, Mr. Higgins?"

"I'm from the Pound—" His voice boomed through the room. "You're the new people—"

"That's right," her mother said. "We don't want a cat. We're getting a dog for Betty."

"I don't want a dog," said Betty desperately. "I want that cat!'   .

"I'll be around in the morning," said Mr. Higgins. "Bright and early! Bright and early," he promised.

✿   ✿   ✿

And then, that night, it happened.

The day had been hot and sultry. Noisy, too, with workmen all over the place. The carpenters were hammering. The electricians were yelling. And the plumbers were upstairs and downstairs, banging away at the pipes.

Finally supper was over and bedtime was here. Betty lay sleepless and unhappy. Tomorrow morning, bright and early, the dogcatcher was coming for the cat. What could she do to keep Calico? Maybe after her mother went to bed, Betty would pack up her little bag and the two of them would run away. Maybe Grandma would take them in and keep Betty as well as the cat.

A full moon swung into place outside her window and brought a golden carpet right into her room. Betty's brown eyes were fixed on the door, waiting for the doorknob to turn. She waited and she waited. No Calico. What was wrong, she wondered? Why didn't Calico come? She was getting so sleepy. Her eyes felt so heavy. She closed them. It took an effort to open them. She closed them again. Then she dropped off to sleep, a deep sleep, a sleep that was different from the sleep of the night before when the apple blossoms tossed their fragrance on her pillow. Tonight she seemed to be sleeping in a sea of black water. Huge waves tossed all about her. She tried to swim. The waves were too high. The sea was too deep. The storm was too strong. She was going down. Down! Down! Down!

Now she came up. Then she went down again. She fought to come up again, to be free of the water's danger. Then the waves turned into sheets and the sheets were being stripped from her body and her face was being scratched by the sharpest of claws and the pillow at her head was being torn open, sending the feathers flying and choking her so she could not cry out. Some sort of leaping creature was jumping on her and would not get down. It kept jumping up and down and pulling at her nightclothes.

"Calico!" she shrieked. "Calico! Stop it! Stop it!"

But Calico went on jumping up and down and purring angrily, with feathers flying around them both. Finally Betty fought free of the cat. She slid from the bed to the floor. Then she smelled it. The room was full of that smell, the strangest sort of smell. It wasn't the odor of the apple blossoms from the tree outside her window. It wasn't the odor of the fragrant grass from the fields beyond the door. It wasn't the odor of the bottle of perfume her father had given her on her birthday. This odor was harsh and unfriendly. This odor made her head swim and her eyes tear and her throat tight.

Suddenly, she knew what it was. *Gas!*

Gas was escaping. It was coming through the floor. It was pouring through the door. It was filling the whole house with its evil odor. Something was wrong. She stumbled to her feet. She ran into the hall. The odor was out in the hall, too. It was all over the house.

She raced across the hallway to her mother's room. The odor filled her mother's room, too, and Betty was a long time shaking her awake. And her mother was even a longer time shaking her father awake.

Anyway, when the dogcatcher arrived in the morning, bright and early as he promised, Mrs. Warren was ready for him.

"You see," she told him, "something went wrong with the plumbing and gas escaped all through the house—and if it weren't for Calico, I wouldn't be here to tell you that I've changed my mind. We're keeping the cat."

"I didn't want a dog," said Betty for the last time. "I wanted that cat!"

The Talking Cat

by Natalie Savage Carlson

ONCE IN ANOTHER TIME, my friends, a great change came into Tante Odette's life although she was already an old woman who thought she had finished with such nonsense as changing one's habits.

It all happened because of a great change that came over Chouchou. The gray cat was a good companion because he seemed quite content to live on bread crusts and cabbage soup. Tante Odette kept a pot of soup boiling on the back of the stove. She added a little more water and a few more cabbage leaves to it each day. In this way, she always had soup on hand and she never had to throw any of it away.

She baked her own bread in her outdoor oven once a week, on Tuesday. If the bread grew stale by Saturday or Sunday, she softened it in the cabbage soup. So nothing was wasted.

As Tante Odette worked at her loom every evening,

Chouchou would lie on the little rug by the stove and steadily stare at her with his big green eyes.

"If only you could talk," Tante Odette would say, "what company you would be for me."

One fall evening, Tante Odette was busy at her loom. Her stubby fingers flew among the threads like pigeons. Thump, thump went the loom.

Suddenly there was a thump, thump that didn't come from the loom. It came from the door.

The old woman took the lamp from the low table and went to the door. She opened it slowly. The light from the lamp shone on a queer old man who had the unmistakable look of the woods. He wore a bright red sash around his waist and a black crow feather in his woolen cap. He had a bushy mustache like a homemade broom and a brown crinkled face.

"Pierre Leblanc at your service," said the old man, making a deep bow.

"What do you want?" asked Tante Odette sharply. "I can't stand here all night with the door open. It wastes heat and firewood."

"I seek shelter and work," answered Pierre Leblanc. "I am getting too old to trap for furs or work in the lumber camps. I would like a job on just such a cozy little place as this."

"I don't need any help," snapped Tante Odette. "I am quite able to do everything by myself. And I have my cat."

She was beginning to close the door, but the man put his gnarled hand against it. He was staring at Chouchou.

"A very smart cat he looks to be," he said. "Why don't you ask him if you should take me in? After all, you need pay me nothing but a roof over my head and a little food."

Tante Odette's eyes grew bigger.

"How ridiculous!" she said. "A cat can't talk. I only wish—"

To her great surprise, Chouchou started to talk.

"Oh, indeed I can," he told her, "if the matter is important enough. This Pierre Leblanc looks to me like a very fine man and a good worker. You should take him in."

Tante Odette stood with her mouth open for two minutes before she could make any sound come out of it. At last she said, "Then come in. It is so rare for a cat to be able to talk that I'm sure one should listen to him when he does."

The old man walked close to the stove and stretched his fingers toward it. He looked at the pot of soup bubbling on the back.

Chouchou spoke again.

"Pierre looks hungry," he said. "Offer him some soup —a big, deep bowl of it."

"Oh, dear," sighed Tante Odette, "at this rate our soup won't last out the week. But if you say so, Chouchou."

Pierre sat at the wooden table and gulped down the soup like a starved wolf. When he had finished, Tante Odette pointed to the loft where he would sleep. Then she took the big gray cat on her lap.

"This is a most amazing thing that you should begin talking after all these years. Whatever came over you?"

But Chouchou had nothing more to say. He covered his nose with the tip of his tail, and there was not another word out of him all night.

Tante Odette decided that the cat's advice had been good. No longer did she have to go to the barn and feed the beasts. And no more skunks crawled into her oven because Pierre saw to it that the door was kept closed. He was indeed a good worker. He seemed quite satisfied with his bed in the loft and his bowls of cabbage soup and chunks of bread.

Only Chouchou seemed to have grown dissatisfied since his arrival.

"Why do you feed Pierre nothing but cabbage soup and bread?" he asked one day. "A workingman needs more food than that. How about some headcheese and pork pie?"

Tante Odette was startled, but Pierre went on drinking his soup.

"But meat is scarce and costs money," she told the cat.

"Pouf!" said the cat. "It is well worth it. Even I am getting a little tired of cabbage soup. A nice pork pie for dinner tomorrow would fill all the empty cracks inside me."

So when Pierre went out to the barn to water the beasts. Tante Odette stealthily lifted the lid of the chest, fished out a torn woolen sock and pulled a few coins out of it. She jumped in surprise when she raised her head and saw Pierre standing in the open doorway watching her.

"I forgot the pail," said Pierre. "I will draw some water from the well while I am about it."

The old woman hastily dropped the lid of the chest and got the pail from behind the stove.

"After Pierre has done his chores," said Chouchou, "he will be glad to go to the store and buy the meat for you."

Tante Odette frowned at the cat.

"But I am the thriftiest shopper in the parish," she said. "I can bring old Henri Dupuis down a few pennies on everything I buy."

"Pierre is a good shopper, too," said Chouchou. "In all Canada, there is not a better judge of meat. Perhaps he will even see something that you would not have thought to buy. Send him to the store."

It turned out that the old man was just as good a shopper as Chouchou had said. He returned from the village with a pinkish piece of pork, a freshly dressed pig's head, a bag of candy and some tobacco for himself.

"But my money," said Tante Odette. "Did you spend all of it?"

"What is money for but to spend?" asked Chouchou from his rug by the stove. "Can you eat money or smoke it in a pipe?"

"No," said Tante Odette.

"Can you put it over your shoulders to keep you warm?"

"No."

"Would it burn in the stove to cook your food?"

"Oh, no, indeed!"

Chouchou closed his eyes.

"Then what good is money?" he asked. "The sooner one gets rid of it, the better."

Tante Odette's troubled face smoothed.

"I never saw it that way before," she agreed. "Of course, you are right, Chouchou. And you are right, too, Pierre, for choosing such fine food."

But when Pierre went out to get a cabbage from the shed, Tante Odette walked to the chest again and counted her coins.

"I have a small fortune, Chouchou," she said. "Now explain to me again why these coins are no good."

But Chouchou had nothing more to say about the matter.

One Tuesday when Pierre Leblanc was cutting trees in the woods and Tante Odette was baking her loaves of bread in the outdoor oven, a stranger came galloping down the road on a one-eyed horse. He stopped in front of the white fence. He politely dismounted and went over to Tante Odette.

The old woman saw at a glance that he was a man of the woods. His blouse was checked and his cap red. Matching it was the red sash tied around his waist. He looked very much like Pierre Leblanc.

"Can you tell me, madame," he asked, "if a man named Pierre Leblanc works here?"

"Yes, he does," answered Tante Odette, "and a very good worker he is."

The stranger did not look satisfied.

"Of course, Canada is full of Pierre Leblancs," he said. "It is a very common name. Does this Pierre Leblanc wear a red sash like mine?"

"So he does," said Tante Odette.

"On the other hand," said the man, "many Pierre Leblancs wear red sashes. Does he have a mustache like a homemade broom?"

"Yes, indeed," said the woman.

"But there must be many Pierre Leblancs with red sashes and mustaches like brooms," continued the stranger. "This Pierre Leblanc who now works for you, can he throw his voice?"

"Throw his voice!" cried Tante Odette. "What witchcraft is that?"

"Haven't you heard of such a gift?" asked the man. "But of course only a few have it—probably only one Pierre Leblanc in a thousand. This Pierre with you, can he throw his voice behind trees and in boxes and up on the roof so it sounds as if someone else is talking?"

"My faith, no!" cried the woman in horror. "I wouldn't have such a one in my house. He would be better company for the *loup-garou*, that evil one who can change into many shapes."

The man laughed heartily.

"My Pierre Leblanc could catch the *loup-garou* in a wolf trap and lead him around by the chain. He is that clever. That is why I am trying to find him. I want him to go trapping with me in the woods this winter. One says that never have there been so many foxes. I need Pierre, for he is smarter than any fox."

The creak of wheels caused them both to turn around. Pierre Leblanc was driving the ox team in from the woods. He stared at the man standing beside Tante Odette. The man stared back at Pierre. Then both men began bouncing on their feet and whooping in their throats. They hugged each other. They kissed each other on the cheek.

"Good old Pierre!"

"Georges, my friend, where have you kept yourself all summer? How did you find me?"

Tante Odette left them whooping and hugging. She walked into the house with a worried look on her face. She sat down at her loom. Finally she stopped weaving and turned to Chouchou.

"I am a little dizzy, Chouchou," she said. "This *loup-garou* voice has upset me. What do you make of it all?"

Chouchou said nothing.

"Please tell me what to do," pleaded Tante Odette. "Shall we let him stay here? It would be very uncomfortable to have voices coming from the roof and the trees."

Chouchou said nothing.

"Is he maybe in league with the *loup-garou?*"

Chouchou said nothing. Tante Odette angrily threw the shuttle at him.

"Where is your tongue?" she demanded. "Have you no words for me when I need them most?"

But if a cat will not speak, who has got his tongue?

Pierre Leblanc came walking in.

"Such a man!" he roared gleefully. "Only the woods are big enough for him."

"Are you going away with him?" asked the woman, not knowing whether she wanted him to say "yes" or "no." If only Chouchou hadn't been so stubborn.

"That makes a problem," said Pierre. "If I go into the woods this winter, it will be cold and I will work like an ox. But there will be much money in my pocket after the furs are sold. If I stay here, I will be warm and comfortable but—"

He pulled his pockets inside out. Nothing fell from them.

"What is this business about your being able to throw your voice to other places?" asked Tante Odette.

"Did Georges say I could do that?"

Tante Odette nodded.

"Ha! Ha!" laughed Pierre. "What a joker Georges is!"

"But perhaps it is true," insisted the woman.

"If you really want to know," said Pierre, "ask Chouchou. He would not lie. Can I throw my voice, Chouchou?"

Chouchou sank down on his haunches and purred.

"Of course not!" he answered. "Whoever heard of such nonsense?"

Tante Odette sighed in relief. Then she remembered that this did not fix everything.

"Will you go with him?" she asked Pierre. "I have

made it very comfortable for you here. And now it is only for supper that we have cabbage soup."

Chouchou spoke up.

"Tante Odette, how can you expect such a good man as Pierre Leblanc to work for only food and shelter? If you would pay him a coin from time to time, he would be quite satisfied to stay."

"But I can't afford that," said the woman.

"Of course you can," insisted Chouchou. "You have a small fortune in the old sock in your chest. Remember what I told you about money?"

"Tell me again," said Tante Odette. "It is hard to hold on to such a thought for long."

"Money is to spend," repeated the cat. "Can it carry hay and water to the beasts? Can it cut down trees for firewood? Can it dig paths through the snow when winter comes?"

"I have caught it again," said Tante Odette. "If you will stay with me, Pierre, I will pay you a coin from time to time."

Pierre smiled and bowed.

"Then I shall be very happy to stay here with you and your wise cat," he decided. "Now I will unload my wood and pile it in a neat stack by the door."

He briskly stamped out. Tante Odette sat down at her loom again.

"We have made a good bargain, haven't we, Chouchou?" She smiled contentedly.

But Chouchou tickled his nose with his tail and said nothing.

That is the way it was, my friends. It would have been a different story if Pierre had not been such a good worker. So remember this: If you must follow the advice of a talking cat, be sure you know who is doing the talking for him.

The Boy Who Drew Cats

by Lafcadio Hearn

A LONG, LONG TIME AGO, in a small country village in Japan, there lived a poor farmer and his wife, who were very good people. They had a number of children and found it very hard to feed them all. The elder son was strong enough when only fourteen years old to help his father, and the little girls learned to help their mother almost as soon as they could walk.

But the youngest child, a little boy, did not seem to be fit for hard work. He was very clever—cleverer than all his brothers and sisters—but he was quite weak and small, and people said he could never grow very big. So his parents thought it would be better for him to become a priest than to become a farmer. They took him with them to the village temple one day and asked the good old priest who lived there if he would have their little boy for his acolyte and teach him all that a priest ought to know.

The old man spoke kindly to the lad, and asked him

some hard questions. So clever were the answers that the priest agreed to take the little fellow into the temple as an acolyte and to educate him for the priesthood.

The boy learned quickly what the old priest taught him and was very obedient in most things. But he had one fault. He liked to draw cats during study hours and to draw cats even where cats ought not to have been drawn at all.

Whenever he found himself alone, he drew cats. He drew them on the margins of the priest's books, and on all the screens of the temple, and on the walls, and on the pillars. Several times the priest told him this was not right, but he did not stop drawing cats. He drew them because he could not really help it. He had what is called "the genius of an artist," and just for that reason he was not quite fit to be an acolyte—a good acolyte should study books.

One day after he had drawn some very clever pictures of cats upon a paper screen, the old priest said to him severely, "My boy, you must go away from this temple at once. You will never make a good priest, but perhaps you will become a great artist. Now let me give you a last piece of advice, and be sure you never forget it: *Avoid large places at night—keep to small!*"

The boy did not know what the priest meant by saying *"Avoid large places—keep to small."* He thought and thought while he was tying up his little bundle of clothes to go away, but he could not understand those words, and he was afraid to speak to the priest any more, except to say good-by.

He left the temple very sorrowfully, and began to wonder what he should do. If he went straight home, he felt sure his father would punish him for having been disobedient to the priest, so he was afraid to go home. All at once he remembered that at the next village, twelve miles away, there was a very big temple. He had heard there were several priests at that temple, and he made up his mind to go to them and ask them to take him for their acolyte.

Now that big temple was closed up, but the boy did not know this fact. The reason it had been closed up was that a goblin had frightened the priests away and had taken possession of the place. Some brave warriors had afterward gone to the temple at night to kill the goblin, but they had never been seen alive again. Nobody had ever told these things to the boy, so he walked all the way to the village hoping to be kindly treated by the priests.

When he got to the village, it was already dark, and all the people were in bed, but he saw the big temple on a hill at the other end of the principal street, and he saw there was a light in the temple. People who tell the story say the goblin used to make that light in order to tempt lonely travelers to ask for shelter. The boy went at once to the temple and knocked. There was no sound inside. He knocked and knocked again, but still nobody came. At last he pushed gently at the door and was quite glad to find that it had not been fastened. So he went in, and saw a lamp burning, but no priest.

He thought some priest would be sure to come very

soon, and he sat down and waited. Then he noticed that everything in the temple was gray with dust and thickly spun over with cobwebs. So he thought to himself that the priests would certainly like to have an acolyte to keep the place clean. He wondered why they had allowed everything to get so dusty. What most pleased him, however, were some big white screens, good to paint cats upon. Though he was tired, he looked at once for a writing box, and found one, and ground some ink, and began to paint cats.

He painted a great many cats upon the screens, and then he began to feel very, very sleepy. He was just on the point of lying down to sleep beside one of the screens, when he suddenly remembered the words: *"Avoid large places—keep to small!"*

The temple was very large, he was all alone, and as he thought of these words—though he could not quite understand them—he began to feel for the first time a little afraid. He resolved to look for a *small place* in which to sleep. He found a little cabinet with a sliding door and went into it and shut himself up. Then he lay down and fell fast asleep.

Very late in the night he was awakened by a most terrible noise—a noise of fighting and screaming. It was so dreadful that he was afraid even to look through a chink of the little cabinet; he lay very still, holding his breath for fright.

The light that had been in the temple went out, but the awful sounds continued and became more awful, and all the temple shook. After a long time, silence came, but the boy was still afraid to move. He did not move until the light of the morning sun shone into the cabinet through the chinks of the little door.

Then he got out of his hiding place very cautiously and looked about. The first thing he saw was that all the floor of the temple was covered with blood. And then he saw, lying dead in the middle of it, an enormous, monstrous rat—a goblin-rat, bigger than a cow!

But who or what could have killed it? There was no man or other creature to be seen. Suddenly the boy observed that the mouths of all the cats he had drawn the night before were red and wet with blood. Then he knew that the goblin had been killed by the cats which he had drawn. And then also, for the first time, he understood why the wise old priest had said to him, *"Avoid large places at night—keep to small."*

Afterward that boy became a very famous artist. Some of the cats which he drew are still shown to travelers in Japan.

The Master Cat, or Puss in Boots

Version by Charles Perrault

ONCE UPON A TIME there was a miller who left no more riches to the three sons he had than his mill, his ass, and his cat. The division was soon made. Neither the lawyer nor the attorney was sent for. They would soon have eaten up all the poor property. The eldest had the mill, the second the ass, and the youngest nothing but the cat.

The youngest, as we can understand, was quite unhappy at having so poor a share.

"My brothers," said he, "may get their living handsomely enough by joining their stocks together; but for my part, when I have eaten up my cat and made me a muff of his skin, I must die of hunger."

The Cat, who heard all this, without appearing to take notice, said to him with a grave and serious air—

"Do not thus afflict yourself, my master; you have nothing else to do but give me a bag and get a pair of boots made for me, that I may scamper through the brambles, and you shall see that you have not so poor a portion in me as you think."

Though the Cat's master did not think much of what he said, he had seen him play such cunning tricks to catch rats and mice—hanging himself by the heels, or hiding himself in the meal to make believe he was dead —that he did not altogether despair of his helping him in his misery. When the Cat had what he asked for, he booted himself very gallantly, and putting his bag about his neck, he held the strings of it in his two forepaws and went into a warren where was a great number of rabbits. He put bran and sow thistle into his bag, and stretching out at length, as if he were dead, he waited for some young rabbits, not yet acquainted with the deceits of the world, to come and rummage his bag for what he had put into it.

Scarcely was he settled when he had what he wanted. A rash and foolish young rabbit jumped into his bag, and Monsieur Puss, immediately drawing close the strings, took him and killed him at once. Proud of his prey, he went with it to the palace and asked to speak with the King. He was shown upstairs into His Majesty's apartment, and making a low bow to the King, he said—

"I have brought you, sire, a rabbit which my noble Lord, the Master of Carabas" (for that was the title which Puss was pleased to give his master) "has commanded me to present to your Majesty from him."

"Tell thy master," said the King, "that I thank him, and that I am pleased with his gift."

Another time he went and hid himself among some standing corn, still holding his bag open; and when a brace of partridges ran into it, he drew the strings, and so caught them both. He then went and made a present of these to the King, as he had done before of the rabbit which he took in the warren. The King, in like manner, received the partridges with great pleasure, and ordered his servants to reward him.

The Cat continued for two or three months thus to carry to His Majesty, from time to time, some of his master's game. One day when he knew that the King was to take the air along the riverside with his daughter, the most beautiful princess in the world, he said to his master—

"If you will follow my advice, your fortune is made. You have nothing else to do but go and bathe in the river, just at the spot I shall show you, and leave the rest to me."

The Marquis of Carabas did what the Cat advised him to, without knowing what could be the use of doing it. While he was bathing, the King passed by, and the Cat cried out with all his might—

"Help! help! My Lord the Marquis of Carabas is drowning!"

At this noise the King put his head out of the coach window, and seeing the cat who had so often brought him game, he commanded his guards to run immediately to the assistance of His Lordship, the Marquis of Carabas.

While they were drawing the poor Marquis out of the river, the Cat came up to the coach and told the King that, while his master was bathing, there came by some rogues, who ran off with his clothes, though he had cried out, "thieves! thieves!" several times, as loud as he could. The cunning Cat had hidden the clothes under a great stone. The King immediately commanded the officers of his wardrobe to run and fetch one of his best suits for the Lord Marquis of Carabas.

The King was extremely polite to him, and as the fine clothes he had given him set off his good looks (for he was well made and handsome), the King's daughter found him much to her liking, and the Marquis of Carabas had no sooner cast two or three respectful and somewhat tender glances than she fell in love with him to distraction. The King would have him come into the coach and take part in the airing. The Cat, overjoyed to see his plan beginning to succeed, marched on before, and meeting with some countrymen who were mowing a meadow, he said to them—

"Good people, you who are mowing, if you do not tell the King that the meadow you mow belongs to my Lord Marquis of Carabas, you shall be chopped as small as herbs for the pot."

The King did not fail to ask the mowers to whom the meadow they were mowing belonged.

"To my Lord Marquis of Carabas," answered they all together, for the Cat's threat had made them afraid.

"You have a good property there," said the King to the Marquis of Carabas.

"You see, sire," said the Marquis, "this is a meadow which never fails to yield a plentiful harvest every year."

The Master Cat, who went still on before, met with some reapers, and said to them—

"Good people, you who are reaping, if you do not say that all this corn belongs to the Marquis of Carabas, you shall be chopped as small as herbs for the pot."

The King, who passed by a moment after, wished to know to whom belonged all that corn, which he then saw.

"To my Lord Marquis of Carabas," replied the reapers,

and the King was very well pleased with it, as well as with the Marquis, whom he congratulated thereupon. The Master Cat, who went always before, said the same thing to all he met, and the King was astonished at the vast estates of my Lord Marquis of Carabas.

Monsieur Puss came at last to a stately castle, the master of which was an Ogre, the richest ever known; for all the lands which the King had then passed through belonged to this castle. The Cat, who had taken care to inform himself who this Ogre was and what he could do, asked to speak with him, saying he could not pass so near his castle without having the honor of paying his respects to him.

The Ogre received him as civilly as an Ogre could and made him sit down.

"I have been assured," said the Cat, "that you have the gift of being able to change yourself into all sorts of creatures you have a mind to; that you can, for example, transform yourself into a lion, or elephant, and the like."

"That is true," answered the Ogre roughly, "and to convince you, you shall see me now become a lion."

Puss was so terrified at the sight of a lion so near him that he immediately climbed into the gutter, not without much trouble and danger, because of his boots, which were no use to him at all for walking upon the tiles. A little while after, when Puss saw that the Ogre had re-sumed his natural form, he came down, and owned he had been very much frightened.

"I have, moreover, been informed," said the Cat, "but

I know not how to believe it, that you also have the power to take on you the shape of the smallest animals; for example, to change yourself into a rat or a mouse, but I must own to you I take this to be impossible."

"Impossible!" cried the Ogre; "you shall see." And at the same time he changed himself into a mouse, and began to run about the floor. Puss no sooner perceived this than he fell upon him and ate him up.

Meanwhile, the King, who saw, as he passed, this fine castle of the Ogre's had a mind to go into it. Puss, who heard the noise of His Majesty's coach coming over the drawbridge, ran out, and said to the King, "Your Majesty is welcome to this castle of my Lord Marquis of Carabas."

"What! My Lord Marquis," cried the King, "and does this castle also belong to you? There can be nothing finer than this courtyard and all the stately buildings which surround it; let us see the interior, if you please."

The Marquis gave his hand to the young Princess and followed the King, who went first. They passed into the great hall, where they found a magnificent collation, which the Ogre had prepared for his friends, who were that day to visit him, but dared not enter, knowing the King was there. His Majesty, charmed with the good qualities of my Lord of Carabas, as was also his daughter, who had fallen violently in love with him, and seeing the vast estate he possessed, said to him—

"It will be owing to yourself only, my Lord Marquis, if you are not my son-in-law."

The Marquis, with low bows, accepted the honor which His Majesty conferred upon him and forthwith that very same day married the Princess.

Puss became a great lord and never ran after mice any more, except for his diversion.

Cats for Kansas

by Le Grand Henderson

TODAY, CATS WALK AMONG the sunflowers in Kansas. But this was not always so, for once there were no cats in Kansas.

This is the story of how cats came to Kansas. This is the story told to the author by descendants of the Kansas pioneers. It is generally agreed that the Kansas pioneers were truthful men.

Once there were no cats in Kansas.

In those days there were buffalo in Kansas. And there were Indians in Kansas.

There were some settlers in Kansas. And old Gabe Slade, the trader, was there, too.

But there were no cats in Kansas.

That was a sad thing for the settlers. Back East, where they came from, there had always been cats to purr around the fireplace and catch the mice and make the house look cozy.

One day Mrs. Gabe Slade said, "Gabe Slade, I want a cat. The Jenkinses want a cat. The Smiths want a cat. The Allens want a cat. And the Joe Greens want a cat. All the settlers in Kansas want a cat. And there are no cats in Kansas."

Gabe Slade, old Gabe Slade, the trader, had an idea. He said, "I will go back East and get some cats. I will bring these cats to Kansas and trade them to the settlers. Then everybody's house will be home sweet home and folks will be happy in Kansas."

So he hitched up his oxen to his covered wagon and he drove across the prairies to the railroad.

He took a train to the river.

Then he went East on Captain Hank Hay's steamboat.

In the East, old Gabe Slade found all the cats he needed. He found black cats and white cats and striped cats and calico cats. He put all these cats into a big wooden crate and he loaded the crate on Captain Hank Hay's steamboat and started back to Kansas.

But there had been no rain for a long time and the river was drying up.

One evening Captain Hank said, "We will have to hurry or we will be stuck in the mud. We will be stuck in the mud all fall and all winter and until the spring floods come. Maybe we will never get unstuck."

Well, there was Gabe Slade, and there were his cats. And way off yonder was Kansas. And still there were no cats in Kansas.

It was a very dark night, and Gabe Slade said, "Captain Hank, how can you see to steer this steamboat through the darkness?"

Captain Hank said, "On a dark night I steer by sound. I steer by the sound of the dogs barking along the shore. I know every dog on this river and I just steer from dog to dog."

Captain Hank listened hard. He said, "There should be a yellow hound dog named William right about here. William barks like a bugle and he always barks when he hears a steamboat."

Gabe Slade and Captain Hank listened, but they heard no bark like a bugle.

If William did not bark, the steamboat could not go on. If the steamboat did not go on, Gabe Slade would not get to Kansas. So there was Gabe Slade, and there were his cats. And way off yonder was Kansas. And still there were no cats in Kansas.

Captain Hank said, "Maybe William is asleep."

Then Gabe Slade had an idea. He got a fishhook and a line and started to fish in the river.

Captain Hank said, "Gabe Slade, this is no time for fishing. This is a time to listen for a yellow hound dog named William."

Gabe Slade went on with his fishing. He pulled in his line and he had a fish. He took the fish off and carried it to his cats.

The cats were hungry. They made the kind of noise that hungry cats make when they see a fish.

And the noise woke the yellow hound dog, whose

name was William. He heard the cats and he started to bark. He barked like a bugle.

Captain Hank heard William. He said, "Now I know where I am," and he started the steamboat.

All the dogs along the river heard Gabe Slade's cats. They all barked, and Captain Hank steered from dog to dog.

And that was how the steamboat got to the railroad by morning.

Gabe Slade put his crate of cats on a train. Then he climbed aboard and started across the prairies to where he had left his covered wagon.

But there were Indians on the prairies in those days. And the Indians did not like the trains, because the trains scared the buffalo and spoiled the Indians' hunting.

So the Indians decided to stop the train. The trains that went to Kansas. Kansas, where there were no cats.

The Indians took a long rope and they stretched it across the railroad tracks. They pulled the rope tight when they saw a train coming. It was the train Gabe Slade and his cats were on.

There were the Indians. And there was the rope. And there was the train. And there was Gabe Slade, and there were his cats. And way off yonder in Kansas were the settlers. And still the settlers had no cats.

Gabe Slade looked out and he saw the rope and he saw the Indians.

He shouted to the engineer.

"Boil up a little more steam," he shouted. "Get her

boiling good and hard. This train must go through, because it's carrying cats for Kansas."

The engineer boiled up as much steam as there was. He went ahead, and the train hit the rope.

The Indians held on to the rope.

Then the air was full of Indians. Indians flew to the right, and Indians flew to the left. And feathers flew all around.

And the train went through.

The train went on to where Gabe Slade had left his covered wagon. Gabe took his cats and he put them in the covered wagon and he started out across the prairie.

Then one day one of the oxen was sick. It was too sick to pull the covered wagon any more.

And there was Gabe Slade with only one ox. And there were the cats, And way off yonder were the settlers. And still the settlers had no cats. No cats in Kansas.

It took two oxen to pull the covered wagon. And now Gabe Slade had only one. One was not enough.

Gabe sat and he thought. He thought and he sat.

He saw some buffalo running across the prairie.

"Mm," he said. "A buffalo is a lot like an ox."

Gabe Slade took a rope and he made a lasso. He went out and lassoed a buffalo.

The buffalo dragged Gabe Slade all over the prairie. It dragged him over the high ground, and it dragged him over the low ground.

It dragged him across a little stream. There were a few trees beside the stream. Gabe Slade tied his rope around a fallen tree.

"There," he said, "I guess that will hold you."

But the buffalo was a very wild buffalo. And he was a very strong buffalo. He dragged the tree across the prairie. The tree had strong branches. The branches dug into the ground like a plow.

The buffalo ran. He turned and he ran. And as he ran, he plowed. He plowed up about a hundred and seven acres. Then he was tired. And when he was tired, he was tamed.

"Well, I do declare," Gabe Slade said. "Now I have a tame buffalo and a hundred and seven acres of good farm land all plowed and ready to plant."

But still the settlers in Kansas had no cats.

Gabe Slade hitched up the tamed buffalo to the covered wagon, along with the good ox.

And he drove his covered wagon across the prairie to Kansas. Kansas where the settlers lived. The settlers who had no cats.

The Jenkinses . . . and the Stewarts . . . and the Joe Greens. And all the other settlers who had no cats.

And when Gabe Slade got to Kansas he traded his cats. He traded them to the Jenkinses . . . and the Smiths . . . and the Allens . . . and the Stewarts . . . and the Joe Greens. And to all the other settlers who had no cats.

Then all the settlers had cats to purr around the fireplace and catch mice and make the house look cozy. Everybody's house was home sweet home. And folks were happy in Kansas.

Old Gabe Slade was happy too. He traded the cats for

seeds. Then he planted the seeds in the hundred and seven acres of land that the buffalo had plowed up.

And that was how Gabe Slade came to have a hundred-and-seven-acre farm, a tame buffalo, and a calico cat.

And that was how cats came to Kansas.

King Solomon's Cat

by Natalia M. Belting

IN THE DAYS when Solomon was king and wore on his finger a ring which gave him the power to understand the language of animals, there dwelt in the king's palace a great golden cat. She was the gift of the Pharaoh of Egypt to Solomon, and in all the world there was no cat such as she. There were those among the king's servants who whispered that she was descended from the Cat Goddess of the Nile, but this they kept from the ears of the king. For Solomon would not have any but the One God worshiped in his kingdom nor would he have tales of other gods carried about in his palace.

Yet the king made much of the golden cat, and because he understood the languages of cats, he carried on many a conversation with her and taught her to sit by his side at the banquet table and hold the candlestick with the lighted candle while he ate. And the king's guests marveled at the sight. But one who came from distant parts, a man from the East named Morolf, disputed the wonder of the cat and said to the king, "My Lord King, you have taught the cat to hold the candlestick. But I can make her forget what you have commanded her."

"Prove it if you can," Solomon challenged.

So when a feast was again ready, Morolf brought, concealed in the sleeve of his robe, three mice. And he sat down at the right hand of the king and gazed upon the cat, who sat as a statue carved from gold and held the great candlestick and the lighted candle to give the king light.

Then Morolf let a mouse slip from his sleeve. Solomon smiled, for the cat moved not at all though the mouse ran across her very paw.

"Ha," Morolf said, seeing the king smile, "one mouse did not tempt her. But let us see what another will do," and he let a second mouse free.

The cat watched the mouse hunt on the table for crumbs. Her eyes followed it the length of the table. But she did not move.

Then the king smiled again, but Morolf let loose the third mouse. And the cat forgot what the king had taught her and dropped the candlestick and chased the mouse and caught it.

And Morolf said to the king, "O Lord King, you cannot change the nature of a cat, though you speak with her and understand her language."

But Solomon answered, "You have proved only,

Morolf, that the wisdom of a king is nothing compared to the wisdom of God. For God created the cat with a purpose and man in his foolishness cannot improve on the work of the Lord. "

The Story of Serapina

by Anne H. White

THIS IS THE STORY of Serapina, a large, handsome, and unusual cat who adopted the Salinus family. It is a story that a great many people did not believe at first, and they said as much to Mrs. Salinus and to the three Salinus children and to Mr. Salinus.

In the beginning, Mrs. Salinus was worried when people suggested that she was exaggerating about Serapina. The children were indignant when people said their stories about the cat were just pretend. Mr. Salinus, however, did not give a fig for what people suggested or what they said. This was because he did not like figs so he did not have any to give. Also, he was a patient man and he simply said, "Wait and see." So people waited. If *you* think the story of Serapina is exaggerated or just pretend, wait and see.

The story of Serapina began, like so many interesting and unusual things, on a perfectly uninteresting and

47

usual day. It was a Tuesday in July, just a plain ordinary Tuesday in a plain ordinary family. Mr. and Mrs. Salinus would not have been any other kind of family for anything in the world. They liked the ordinary block of ordinary white houses and green yards where they lived. Mr. Salinus liked his wife and his children and his job, and Mrs. Salinus liked her husband and her children and parts of her job. Her job was being a mother, cook, laundress, dressmaker, sock-darner, trained nurse, arithmetic tutor, baseball player, sitter, and a few other things. The parts she didn't like were the baseball playing part because she was always put out at once and the sitter part because she never went out at all. Mrs. Salinus was a very anxious mother. She was always worrying about the children and she was very cautious about sitters.

On this particular Tuesday, Mr. and Mrs. Salinus got up as usual when the alarm went off at six forty-five. Mr. Salinus put on his bathrobe and slippers, made a noise in his throat which meant, "Good morning, my dear, I hope you slept well." It sounded like "Gamungameer. Hoeya slipple," but Mrs. Salinus understood. She nodded and yawned and put on her bathrobe and slippers. Then they washed their faces, got dressed, and separated, Mrs. Salinus going to the kitchen and Mr. Salinus going his rounds. First he woke his daughter Sally, who was twelve years old and a very sound sleeper. Then he got his son Peter up. Peter, who was ten, was always reading instead of getting dressed. Then Mr. Salinus found his son Bobby, who was going-on-five and was always hiding somewhere. This morning he found Bobby in the bottom of the clothes hamper. Finally Mr. Salinus went downstairs into the kitchen, where Mrs. Salinus was frying eggs and looking rather cross.

Mr. Salinus fetched in the milk bottles from the back porch, got the oranges from the vegetable bin, the butter and jam from the refrigerator, and the bread from the breadbox. Then he looked at his wife.

"What is the matter?" he asked. "You look rather cross."

"I have plenty of reason to be cross once in a while," Mrs. Salinus snapped. And she slapped the eggs over so hard some fat splashed onto her hand. "Ouch!" she exclaimed. "Please tell the children breakfast is ready."

Mr. Salinus called the children, Mrs. Salinus dished up the eggs, and gradually the family sat down to breakfast. Sally had forgotten to brush her hair again and had to be sent back upstairs; Peter had forgotten to wash his face and was also sent back; and Bobby could not be found for some time because he was hiding in the pots-and-pans cupboard. But finally breakfast began, and Mr. Salinus asked Mrs. Salinus why she was cross.

"It's the same old story," Mrs. Salinus said with a sigh. "I just never have a minute to myself. There is a Garden Club lecture I should like to go to, there is the Dorcas Society Sewing Social, and it is so long since we have played any bridge I have forgotten how."

"You could teach us how to play," Peter suggested. "Then we could stay up until the middle of the night and play with you."

"Can I too?" Bobby asked because he was often left out of things. Mrs. Salinus laughed and said she would not teach any of them how to play bridge for a long time.

"I am being very horrid and complaining," she admitted. "I wish we could go out in the evening once in a while."

Mr. Salinus also would have liked to go out in the evening once in a while, but he did not say so. He knew how anxious his wife was about the children. So he tried to cheer her up by telling her that in ten years the children would be old enough to be left alone and then he and she could go out every night in the week. But Mrs. Salinus thought by that time she would be too old and too tired to stir from her fireside.

The Salinus breakfast ended and the children rushed from the dining room, forgetting their vitamins, and went out into the yard to play. It was a very nice yard with three trees, a flower bed, a sand pile, a hammock, and a picket fence all around it.

"Please shut the front door," Mrs. Salinus called to Sally. "It is fearfully blowy today."

Mr. Salinus left through the back door for the garage, and Mrs. Salinus asked him to shut that door because of the high wind. Then she cleared the table, did the dishes, tidied the upstairs, and came down for her second cup of coffee before she tackled the downstairs. While she stood before the window watching the children and drinking her coffee, she had a funny feeling that someone was watching her from behind. How silly, she told herself. There is no one in the house because both the doors have been shut all morning. And there are full screens on all the windows. But, in spite of herself, she turned her head—and looked right into the large, unblinking eyes of an enormous cat. The cat was sitting straight up on the hearthrug, its front paws neatly together, its tail wound across them. It was staring at Mrs. Salinus in a very curious manner, as though it could not decide if it liked what it saw or not. Mrs. Salinus noticed that it had one green eye and one blue eye.

"Well!" she exclaimed, "where on earth did you come from?"

The cat winked slowly with its green eye. The wink was neither friendly nor gay but a sort of thoughtful wink, or an undecided one-eyed squint. Mrs. Salinus, who did not like cats as a rule, decided the children must have put the cat in the house. She finished her coffee and started her downstairs work. She tried to ignore the cat, but this she found difficult because it watched her so closely as she did her chores.

When she went to the kitchen to get the children's eleven o'clock milk and cookies, the cat followed her, and it was under the piano when she played a scale to remind Sally to come in and practice. Sally did not notice the cat, and her mother wisely did not mention it at practice time. Then there was lunch to get, and Mrs. Salinus forgot all about the cat until dessert.

"Did you let your cat out?" she asked the children as she spooned raspberry jello into Bobby.

"What a silly question!" Sally exclaimed in a superior manner. "We haven't any cat."

"There was one in the house all morning," Mrs. Salinus replied.

"And you never told us!" Sally cried reproachfully. "I love cats. I wonder where it is."

"Well," Peter informed her through a mouthful of gingersnaps, "you don't have to wonder. It is right outside behind you, looking in the window."

All three children rushed to the window, and, sure enough, there was the cat staring in at them in that very curious manner.

"Come and finish your milk, children," Mrs. Salinus told them. "No cat until after lunch." In about one minute it was after lunch and the children all dashed for the door. They stopped so suddenly, however, that they fell over one another. Sitting in the doorway between the dining room and the living room was the enormous cat, its front paws neatly together and its tail wound across them. By the time the children had untangled themselves it had disappeared.

"Don't frighten the cat, children," Mrs. Salinus warned them. "It will scratch you."

"But it has gone away!" Bobby cried in great disappointment.

"Then come take your nap," his mother suggested. "And when you wake up perhaps it will be back."

"There it is!" Peter shouted, dashing over to the window that looked out onto the front steps. "It's outdoors again."

The whole family rushed to the window, and there was

the cat, sitting on the broad, brick step before the front
door, which was firmly shut.

At this moment Mrs. Salinus felt some very tingly
prickles run up her spine and swirl around in the back
of her head. She knew they were what she called her
trouble-ahead prickles because she always got them
before something upsetting happened.

"Wait!" she commanded the children, who were start-
ing for the front door. "There is something very peculiar
about this cat. How did it get in and out this morning,
and how did it get in and out now? The doors and windows are not open because it is too windy."

"Maybe it's a magic cat!" Peter always hoped that
things would be better than they seemed to be. "Maybe
it can walk through doors and windows like ghosts."

"Don't be silly," Sally told him. Sally hoped things
might be better, too, but she never admitted it out loud.
"You can't see ghosts and you can see that cat. And there
are no magic cats, are there, Mummy?"

Mrs. Salinus opened her mouth to say no, in spite of
the prickles, when the cat unwound its tail from across
its neat front paws.

It did not uncurl its tail the way most cats do, but unwound it, not once but twice. Then it flipped the tail
out behind on the brick step, and the children saw that
it was marked by very black rings of fur which divided it
into sections like a bamboo pole. The cat changed the
number of these sections whenever it wanted to by
twitching its tail. Sometimes the tail was quite short and

thick, with only a few sections showing, and sometimes it was long and thin, with a great many sections showing. It really seemed to be a telescoping tail.

After the cat had flipped its tail out long, medium, and short, it began to do other exercises. It crooked the tip over to make a little hook, a big hook, an S hook, and finally it arched its tail over its back and dusted off its nose with the tip. It then curled the tip over and rolled its tail up in a neat, nautical coil. Finished with that, the cat rose to its feet and stretched. It seemed to the Salinus family to get bigger and bigger in all directions until it looked nearly as big as a cocker spaniel or a fox terrier. Then it shook itself and became a perfectly normal-sized cat with a perfectly normal-sized tail hanging down behind.

Mrs. Salinus and the children were too astonished to move or speak. While they remained glued to the window, the cat strolled over to the front door. With just a hint of showing off, a sort of "watch-this-one" swagger, it squinted at the door latch first with one eye and then with the other, adjusted its tail in two twitches, lifted it, crooked the tip over the latch, and leaned. The door opened, the cat walked in, the door closed. The cat appeared in the living room, where it sat down and calmly began to straighten out its fur.

"It *is* a magic cat!" Peter yelled with delight.

"No," Sally insisted. "It's probably a trained cat."

"Make it do some more," Bobby begged, forgetting that no one had made the cat do anything.

Mrs. Salinus did not say a word. She wished that she did not see the cat sitting right there in front of her. If she did not see it, perhaps she could believe she had not seen it open the door or do those things with its tail. Mrs. Salinus was a sensible woman and she knew perfectly well that cats don't open doors and don't have adjustable tails. She found it very upsetting to see a cat do things a cat does not do. Peter and Sally and Bobby were not at all upset. They were curious, which is a much better thing to be.

"Perhaps it has an elastic tail," Peter suggested as the children stared at the cat. "I will just see if it pulls out."

And he stooped down to pull the cat's tail. He was going to pull it very gently, just enough to see if it did pull, because Peter liked to find out what things did and did not do. The cat continued to arrange its fur but, as Peter's hand reached down, it flicked its tail up sharply. Peter jumped back with a yelp.

"It's an iron tail!" he exclaimed. "It's not an elastic tail at all!"

Sally and Bobby then did just what you or I would have done. They reached down to see what Peter meant, and they saw. The cat rapped them smartly over the knuckles, rose, and went upstairs.

The family followed the cat, who went straight into Bobby's room and jumped onto the window seat.

"There, now," Mrs. Salinus said. "You see, the kitty knows it is time for you to take a nap, Bobby. It is waiting for you to get into bed." Mrs. Salinus did not believe one word of what she said, but she thought she would just pretend, to amuse Bobby.

"Then why doesn't it pull down my blinds?" Bobby asked, always willing to pretend, especially at nap time.

The cat had noticed the venetian blind cord and was batting it gently with a front paw. As Bobby spoke, the cat jerked the cord and down came the blind. The cat then left the room.

"Now wasn't that a coincidence!" exclaimed Mrs. Salinus, whipping the covers up over Bobby and hurrying the other two children out of the room. "Go to sleep, Bobby, and when you wake up you can play with the kitty if it is still here."

Mrs. Salinus earnestly hoped that the cat would not be there when Bobby woke up. She had enough of that cat. It was queer, doing those things with its tail, and opening doors, and lowering venetian blinds. That business with the blind was pure accident, she told herself. But it made her uneasy; in fact she was really upset.

"Mummy," Peter asked her when she joined the children in the living room, "what is a coincidence exactly?"

"Oh, goodness!" Sally remarked in her superior voice, because she was rather inclined to act superior at times, "I know that. If I called and called the cat and it did not come, that would not be a coincidence. But if I said I wish the cat would come here and play with us, and it came, that would be a concidence."

Mrs. Salinus pretended she did not hear a deep, rumbling purr, and see the cat appear from nowhere and stretch out at Sally's feet.

Peter considered the cat thoughtfully. "Well, you did say so, and it came," he said. "Is that a coincidence, Mummy?"

"Yes, yes, of course." Mrs. Salinus wished she was as positive as she pretended. "Certainly. What else could it be? Cats can't understand English. Besides, she was not around when Sally spoke."

Peter was delighted at the possibilities offered by this wonderful cat. He suggested that it might be an eavesdropping cat who made a practice of staying out of sight and listening to what people were saying.

"Why would it do that?" Sally asked impatiently. "Eavesdropping is usually very dull. It might be a mind-reading cat, though, like those people who can tell what you are thinking without being told."

"Nonsense!" Their mother's voice sound scared. "I never heard of a mind-reading cat and I don't think I want to."

Peter and Sally thought a mind-reading cat would be fun and they tried hard to make the cat read their minds. It was not at all interested even in trying and curled up on the sofa for a snooze.

Mrs. Salinus decided she was being very foolish about the cat, which must be a trained or circus cat with an unusual tail. Some people, for instance, could turn their elbows all the way round or pull back their thumbs to touch their wrists. And there were acrobats who could turn themselves inside out. Perhaps it was an acrobat cat. Certainly it was unusual. She thought she had better let the police know right off that she had a strange cat in the house.

"I am going to telephone the ploice that we have found a stray cat," she told the children. When she spoke the words "a stray cat" the cat sprang off the sofa, making a protesting noise in its throat, stalking into the dining room, and banged the door behind it in what was unmistakably a huff.

"But, Mummy," Peter insisted, "it would not be at all true to say we 'found' a cat. We did *not* find it. It found us. It came right to our door when it could have gone to anyone else's on the whole block."

"Even if it did find us—and, mind you, I think it was

just chance—we can't keep it." Mrs. Salinus spoke very firmly. "Animals can't choose people, you know. It's the other way round."

"When I grow up I shall change it so they *can* choose people if they want to," Sally remarked. Sally had a long list of things she was going to change when she grew up, and it irritated her that growing up took so long.

"Unfortunately," her mother replied, "while you are waiting to grow up I shall have to telephone about the cat."

She went to the telephone to call the police but changed her mind before she picked up the receiver. She would wait, she decided, for Mr. Salinus to come home. She could hardly expect the police to believe her if she said she had a cat that opened doors with its tail. Cats, she kept telling herself, don't do things like that.

So she waited until Mr. Salinus returned from his office. Then his whole family told him all about the extraordinary cat, everyone talking at once. The cat sat directly opposite him, staring at him out of its blue eye and its green eye. Mr. Salinus stared back and listened to his wife and to his children at the same time. He did not agree with his wife about cats. He liked them as a rule, the way he liked most things, and therefore he understood them.

"Well, Serapina," he said at last to the cat when there was a pause in the conversation, "you seem to have created some excitement around here."

The cat winked, this time with its blue eye, and the

wink was friendly and a tiny bit gay. Its black whiskers turned up slightly at the same time but no one except Mr. Salinus noticed this.

"How do you know its name *is* Serapina?" Mrs. Salinus asked.

"I don't know," Mr. Salinus replied. "I just sort of feel it is."

"I told you, Mummy!" Sally exclaimed excitedly. "It is a mind-reading cat and it is reading its name right into Daddy's brain."

Mr. Salinus laughed and would have liked to discuss the idea with Sally but Mrs. Salinus interrupted.

"Nonsense!" she exploded nervously. "Whatever it is, I don't want it here. I don't want a cat putting ideas into my mind, or reading it either. I won't have a cat sitting around and thinking I don't know *what* about me and listening to everything I say!"

"Now, now, dear." Mr. Salinus spoke soothingly. "Why should you care what it *thinks* as long as it doesn't *say* anything? The cat who is never catty!" Mr. Salinus was only trying to amuse Mrs. Salinus, but, although Sally and Peter thought their father very funny, Mrs. Salinus did not think so.

"I refuse to have anything to do with that animal," she insisted. "And I want you to write to the paper immediately."

She marched across the room to her desk, picked up a piece of paper and a pencil, and brought them to her husband.

Mr. Salinus was a very obliging man so he took the

paper and pencil in spite of loud protests from his children. "Perhaps no one will answer the ad," he told them as he gnawed the eraser, thinking what to say.

"Just say, 'Found: a stray, speckled cat,'" Mrs. Salinus suggested.

At these words Serapina, for that was her name ever after, let out a sharp, indignant snarl, lifted up her tail, and brought it down smartly on Mrs. Salinus's instep. Mrs. Salinus cried "Ouch!" and Mr. Salinus looked at her reprovingly.

"You have hurt her feelings," he told his wife. "I shall say, 'Found: an unusual, large, and handsome multicolored cat with black whiskers.'"

As he wrote these words down Serapina bunched herself at his feet and rolled soft, quick drums deep inside her. Mr. Salinus finished writing and stuck the paper in his pocket to be mailed in the morning. Then he leaned down and rubbed Serapina's ears.

"Well, well," he remarked, "you *are* an interesting addition to the family and we shall certainly be sorry to lose you."

Serapina tilted her wide face back so she could look at Mr. Salinus. She smirked her whiskers and narrowed both eyes at him in a look that said clearly, "Don't count your chickens before they are hatched."

The Cat with the Crooked Tail

by Frances Carpenter

IN OTHER TIMES, in the Far Eastern land of Siam, the king of the country was treated like a god.

"Brother of the Moon!"

"Master of One Thousand Elephants!"

"Lord of Four and Twenty Golden Umbrellas!"

These are only a few of the splendid names the people of old Siam gave their King.

No one dared come before the King's throne, except he crawled on the ground. When the Brother of the Moon came out of his shining palace, he rode in a gold chair, carried high on the shoulders of a dozen strong men.

All along the King's way people knelt down. They bumped their heads on the ground before him. No one dared to lift his eyes to look at this mighty monarch.

In all that ancient kingdom, there was only one who

always stood up, straight and proud, before the King. Only one dared to look into the face of the Half Brother of the Sun. And that one was a cat!

Siamese cats of those ancient times were very much like the Siamese cats of today. Their silky coats were pale gold. Their ear tips, their tails, their four paws, and their faces were like shining brown velvet. And their proud eyes were as blue as the very heavens above.

Oh, the Siamese cat was a royal animal. People in Siam knew this well. These pale-gold, blue-eyed cats were not for the common folk. Only in the palaces of the King, or perhaps in the house of a prince, were these noble cats to be seen.

"When God made our cat," Siamese grandmothers told the children, "he took the grace of the tiger. He took the sweetness of the lovebird, the beauty of the young deer, and the softness of the dove. He took the quickness of the lightning and the wisdom of the elephant. All these fine things he put together when he made the blue-eyed, golden cat."

"But in one way that first cat was not like our cats today," the wise old grandmothers said. "That first cat had no crook at the end of his brown tail."

The old grandmothers knew why this was. Or they said they did. And they told this story to explain how the Siamese cat came to have a crooked tail.

It happened so long ago that no one knows really how long ago it was. But there was once a certain King of Siam. A great king was he. Truly he was a king fit to be called "Half Brother of the Sun." Truly he was Master of One Thousand Elephants.

In this great King's royal stable there were more elephants than you could count in one day. Some were the precious "white" elephants which only kings may ride upon.

These royal beasts were not exactly white. But they had patches of white upon their huge ears. And their small eyes were light instead of dark.

White elephants like these were rare in the Siamese jungles. They were the greatest treasures any king could have.

Yet even more than his white elephants did this King prize his favorite Siamese cat. By night the cat slept upon his master's royal bed. And each morning, when the sun rose, it was a soft brown furry paw on his cheek that wakened the King.

By day the cat sat close to his master's side. His silken cushion lay at the foot of the King's golden throne.

You may think it was strange to have a cat in a throne room. Indeed it was odd, especially in such a throne room as that of this King. For it was a bright, shining room. Golden bushes and trees were set along its walls. Their trunks and their branches were only gilded. But their twigs and leaves were pure gold.

The King's throne was gold, too. His pointed gold crown, with its flashing gems, sat high on his head, like a tiny temple. Of gold also was the splendid nine-storied umbrella which was above the King's throne. Gold and rich jewels adorned the King's clothes. His pointed red shoes were embroidered in gold.

The cat, too, wore gold. A fine chain of gold, sparkling with gems, lay around his soft throat. Another gold chain was fastened into this cat's kingly collar. Its end was linked to a ruby ring which the King wore on his thumb.

Even today Siamese cats know how to talk to their masters. Speak to your own Siamese cat, and he will answer. Be silent too long and he will rub his soft body against your foot. Then he will begin to talk, all by himself, in his low, deep, cat voice.

Well, it was like that also so long ago. Only in those times people could understand the words which their cats spoke.

"No human in all my kingdom is so wise as you, my dear Cat." The King often said these words, as his royal hand stroked the cat's head. Often and often that King asked his cat to tell him what he should do.

Sometimes a hunter would bring a baby white elephant in from the jungle. The hunter would then crawl before the King to receive his reward. Lying flat on the ground before the golden throne, he would hear the King speak to the cat.

"What shall we give this good hunter of elephants, O Wise Cat?"

The man's heart would be glad when he heard the cat say, "Give him ten thousand silver ticals, O King! Give him ten thousand bags of rice, too! A white elephant is without price."

Or it might have been a very bad man who came crawling in.

"How shall we punish this wicked man, O Cat?" the King would ask.

The cat would rub his head with his paw, and he would reply, "Put the iron collar about his neck. Put chains on his legs. Make him a slave!" Oh, that cat had no mercy on people who did not do right.

Now, it happened one day that this Siamese King was taken sick. The royal doctors shook their heads. They could not find out what was the matter with the Lord of the Golden Umbrellas.

"It may be that the Brother of the Moon needs a good rest," they said. "Perhaps your Heavenly Majesty will go in the royal houseboat to your summer palace up the river. The country air may cure your sickness."

The royal houseboat took the King and the cat up the broad Menam River. But there, in the peace and fresh air of the up-country, the King was no better.

"It may be the summer heat is causing the King's sickness. Let the Ruler of the Ocean Tides go down in his glass palace under the lake," the doctors next ordered. With his cat by his side, the King took his seat inside the great box of glass. Its door was closed tight. No water could come in.

Down, down in the cool lake the glass room was dropped. The King's servants tended him well. The air was somehow kept sweet and fresh. The summer heat did not find its way to the cool bottom of the lake. Fish swam past the glass house. They amused the King well.

Yet his sickness did not go away. And he came back to his splendid palace.

The doctors shook their heads harder. "It must be poison!" they said. "Someone is putting poison into the King's drinking cup. It can be nothing else."

They set guards beside the golden goblet from which the King always drank. By day and by night the guards were there. But at some time or other those guards must have slept. The King grew sicker and sicker.

Then the King's wives took their turn. Each night ten of his youngest wives sat beside the table upon which the golden goblet was placed. But they, too, must have slept. The King grew worse and worse.

"Something must be done quickly," the doctors said, "or our King will die."

"Let me watch over the King's cup," the blue-eyed cat said at last.

"How could you keep awake, Sir Cat?" The doctors shook their heads. They knew how well cats like to nap. They knew how often the King's cat dozed on the silken cushion at his master's feet.

But the King heard the cat's request.

"My wise cat shall guard my cup." The King gave the order.

So they lifted the cat up onto the table. There, he lay down close beside the great golden goblet.

For a day and a night, for another day and another night, the cat's blue eyes stayed open. Then his eyelids began to close. He knew he could not keep them open very much longer.

"If only I could take just one little nap," the cat said to himself. "I will wind the end of my tail around the foot of the King's goblet. Should the goblet be moved, I shall surely feel it."

The cat's smoky-brown tail curled itself tight around the thin golden base of the King's cup. Day after day, his tail never let go, except when the King wanted to drink.

In all that great palace there was no man so bold that he would dare now to come near the goblet of the King. Well did all know that at the rustle of their clothes the cat would spring up into the air. Sharp claws would rake any arm near enough to drop poison into the King's cup.

Little by little, the King began to feel better. With the poison gone from his goblet, he soon was well again. At last there was no longer any reason to keep watch over his cup.

Everyone cried out, "Long live the Cat! He has saved our Lord and Master."

The King took the pussy up into his lap. He stroked his velvety back. He softly pulled the dark tail. It was then that the King felt the crook that had come into the tail of his faithful cat. So long had the cat's tail been curled around the cup, that it could not now unbend.

Never did this little crook disappear from the tail of the King's cat. It appeared in the tails of his kittens. His grand-kittens and his great-grand-kittens had crooked tails, too.

Siamese cats were proud of the little crook in the ends

of their tails. They said it proved they were of the same family as this famous cat that saved the life of a king.

From that time on a Siamese cat with a crooked tail was the most highly prized. It is only in other lands, far, far from Siam, that people do not care whether or not their cats have crooked tails.

The Cat Who Went to Heaven

by Elizabeth Coatsworth

ONCE UPON A TIME, far away in Japan, a poor young artist sat alone in his little house, waiting for his dinner. His housekeeper had gone to market, and he sat sighing to think of all the things he wished she would bring home. He expected her to hurry in at any minute, bowing and opening her little basket to show him how wisely she had spent their few pennies. He heard her step and jumped up. He was very hungry!

But the housekeeper lingered by the door, and the basket stayed shut.

"Come," he cried, "what is in that basket?"

The housekeeper trembled and held the basket tight in two hands. "It has seemed to me, sir," she said, "that we are very lonely here." Her wrinkled face looked humble and obstinate.

"Lonely!" said the artist. "I should think so! How can

we have guests when we have nothing to offer them? It is so long since I have tasted rice cakes that I forget what they taste like!" And he sighed again, for he loved rice cakes, and dumplings, and little cakes filled with sweet bean jelly. He loved tea served in fine china cups, in company with some friend, seated on flat cushions, talking perhaps about a spray of peach blossoms standing like a little princess in an alcove. But weeks and weeks had gone by since anyone had bought even the smallest picture. The poor artist was glad enough to have rice and a coarse fish now and then. If he did not sell another picture soon, he would not have even that. His eyes went back to the basket. Perhaps the old woman had managed to pick up a turnip or two, or even a peach, too ripe to haggle long over.

"Sir," said the housekeeper, seeing the direction of his look, "it has often seemed to me that I was kept awake by rats."

At that the artist laughed out loud.

"Rats?" he repeated. "Rats? My dear old woman, no rats come to such a poor house as this where not the smallest crumb falls to the mats."

Then he looked at the housekeeper and a dreadful suspicion filled his mind.

"You have brought us home nothing to eat!" he said.

"True, master," said the old woman sorrowfully.

"You have brought us home a cat!" said the artist.

"My master knows everything!" answered the house-keeper, bowing low.

Then the artist jumped to his feet and strode up and down the room and pulled his hair, and it seemed to him that he would die of hunger and anger.

"A cat? A cat?" he cried. "Have you gone mad? Here we are starving and you must bring home a goblin, a goblin to share the little we have, and perhaps to suck our blood at night! Yes! It will be fine to wake up in the dark and feel teeth at our throats and look into eyes as big as lanterns! But perhaps you are right! Perhaps we are so miserable it would be a good thing to have us die at once and be carried over the ridgepoles in the jaws of a devil!"

"But master, master, there are many good cats, too!" cried the poor old woman. "Have you forgotten the little boy who drew all the pictures of cats on the screens of the deserted temple and then went to sleep in a closet and heard such a racket in the middle of the night? And in the morning, when he awoke again, he found the giant rat lying dead, master—the rat who had come to kill him! Who destroyed the rat, sir, tell me that? It was his own cats, there they sat on the screen as he had drawn them, but there was blood on their claws! And he became a great artist like yourself. Surely, there are many good cats, master."

Then the old woman began to cry. The artist stopped and looked at her as the tears fell from her bright black eyes and ran down the wrinkles in her cheeks. Why should he be angry? He had gone hungry before.

"Well, well," he said, "sometimes it is good fortune to have even a devil in the household. It keeps other devils away. Now I suppose this cat of yours will wish to eat. Perhaps it may arrange for us to have some food in the house. Who knows? We can't be worse off than we are."

The housekeeper bowed very low in gratitude.

"There is not a kinder heart in the whole town than my master's," she said, and prepared to carry the covered basket into the kitchen.

But the artist stopped her. Like all artists he was curious.

"Let us see the creature," he said, pretending he scarcely cared whether he saw it or not.

So the old woman put down the basket and opened the lid. Nothing happened for a moment. Then a round, pretty white head came slowly above the bamboo, and two big yellow eyes looked about the room, and a little white paw appeared on the rim. Suddenly, without moving the basket at all, a little white cat jumped out on the mats, and stood there as a person might stand who scarcely knew if she were welcome. Now that the cat was out of the basket, the artist saw that she had yellow and black spots on her sides, a little tail like a rabbit's, and that she did everything daintily.

"Oh, a three-colored cat," said the artist. "Why didn't you say so from the beginning? They are very lucky, I understand."

As soon as the little cat heard him speak so kindly, she walked over to him and bowed down her head as though she were saluting him, while the old woman clapped her hands for joy. The artist forgot that he was

hungry. He had seen nothing so lovely as their cat for a
long time.

"She will have to have a name," he declared, sitting
down again on the old matting, while the cat stood
sedately before him. "Let me see: she is like new snow
dotted with gold pieces and lacquer; she is like a white
flower on which butterflies of two kinds have alighted;
she is like—"

But here he stopped. For a sound like a teakettle
crooning on the fire was filling his little room.

"How contented!" sighed the artist. "This is better

than rice." Then he said to the housekeeper, "We have been lonely, I see now."

"May I humbly suggest," said the housekeeper, "that we call this cat Good Fortune?"

Somehow the name reminded the artist of all his troubles.

"Anything will do," he said, getting up and tightening his belt over his empty stomach, "but take her to the kitchen now, out of the way." No sooner were the words out of his mouth than the little cat rose, and walked away, softly and meekly.

✿   ✿   ✿

The next morning the artist found the cat curled up in a ball on his cushion.

"Ah! the softest place, I see!" said he. Good Fortune immediately rose and, moving away, began to wash herself with the greatest thoroughness and dexterity. When the housekeeper came back from market and cooked the small meal, Good Fortune did not go near the stove, though her eyes wandered toward it now and then and her thistle-down whiskers quivered slightly with hunger. She happened to be present when the old woman brought in a low table and set it before her master. Next came a bowl of fish soup—goodness knows how the housekeeper must have wheedled to get that fish!—but Good Fortune made a point of keeping her eyes in the other direction.

"One would say," said the artist, pleased by her behavior, "that she understood it is not polite to stare at

people while they eat. She has been very properly
brought up. From whom did you buy her?"

"I bought her from a fisherman in the market," said
the old woman. "She is the eldest daughter of his chief
cat. You know a junk never puts out to sea without a cat
to frighten away the water devils."

"Pooh!" said the artist. "A cat doesn't frighten devils.
They are kin. The sea demons spare a ship out of cour-
tesy to the cat, not from fear of her."

The old woman did not contradict. She knew her place
better than that. Good Fortune continued to sit with her
face to the wall.

The artist took another sip or two of soup. Then he
said to the housekeeper, "Please be kind enough to bring
a bowl for Good Fortune when you bring my rice. She
must be hungry."

When the bowl came he called her politely. Having
been properly invited, Good Fortune stopped looking
at the other side of the room and came to sit beside her
master. She took care not to eat hurriedly and soil her
white round chin. Although she must have been very
hungry, she would eat only half her rice. It was as though
she kept the rest for the next day, wishing to be no more
of a burden than she could help.

So the days went. Each morning the artist knelt quietly
on a mat and painted beautiful little pictures that no one
bought—some of warriors with two swords, some of
lovely ladies doing up their long curtains of hair, some
of the demons of the wind blowing out their cheeks,
and some little laughable ones of rabbits running in the

moonlight, or fat badgers beating on their stomachs like drums. While he worked, the old woman went to market with a few of their remaining pennies; she spent the rest of her time in cooking, washing, scrubbing, and darning to keep their threadbare house and their threadbare clothes together. Good Fortune, having found that she was unable to help either of them, sat quietly in the sun, ate as little as she could, and often spent hours with lowered head before the image of the Buddha on its low shelf.

"She is praying to the Enlightened One," said the housekeeper in admiration.

"She is catching flies," said the artist. "You would believe anything wonderful of your spotted cat." Perhaps he was a little ashamed to remember how seldom he prayed now when his heart felt so heavy.

But one day he was forced to admit that Good Fortune was not like other cats. He was sitting in his special room watching the sparrows fly in and out of the hydrangea bushes outside, when he saw Good Fortune leap from a shadow and catch a bird. In a second the brown wings, the blackcapped head, the legs like briers, the frightened eyes, were between her paws. The artist would have clapped his hands and tried to scare her away, but before he had time to make the least move, he saw Good Fortune hesitate and then slowly, slowly, lift first one white paw and then another from the sparrow. Unhurt, in a loud whir of wings, the bird flew away.

"What mercy!" cried the artist, and the tears came into his eyes. Well he knew his cat must be hungry and well he knew what hunger felt like. "I am ashamed when I think that I called such a cat a goblin," he thought. "Why, she is more virtuous than a priest."

It was just then, at that very moment, that the old housekeeper appeared, trying hard to hide her excitement.

"Master!" she said as soon as she could find words. "Master! The head priest from the temple himself is here in the next room and wishes to see you. What, oh what, do you think His Honor has come here for?"

"The priest from the temple wishes to see me?" repeated the artist, scarcely able to believe his ears, for the priest was a very important person, not one likely to spend his time in visiting poor artists whom nobody thought much of. When the housekeeper nodded her head until it nearly fell off, the artist felt as excited as she did, but he forced himself to be calm.

"Run! run!" he exclaimed. "Buy tea and cakes," and he pressed into the old woman's hands the last thing of value he owned, the vase which stood in the alcove of his room and always held a branch or spray of flowers. But even if his room must be bare after this, the artist did not hesitate; no guest could be turned away without proper entertainment. He was ashamed to think that he had kept the priest waiting for even a minute and had not seen him coming and welcomed him at the door. He scarcely felt Good Fortune rub encouragingly against his ankles as he hurried off.

In the next room the priest sat, lost in meditation. The artist bowed low before him, drawing in his breath politely, and then waited to be noticed. It seemed to him a century before the priest lifted his head and the far-off look went out of his eyes. Then the artist bowed again and said that his house was honored forever by so holy a presence.

The priest wasted no time in coming to the point.

"We desire," said he, "a painting of the death of our Lord Buddha for the temple. There was some discussion as to the artist, so we put slips of paper, each marked with a name, before the central image in the great hall, and in the morning all the slips had blown away but yours. So we knew Buddha's will in the matter. Hearing something of your circumstances, I have brought a first payment with me so that you may relieve your mind of worry while at your work. Only a clear pool has beautiful reflections. If the work is successful, as we hope, your fortune is made, for what the temple approves becomes the fashion in the town." With that the priest drew a heavy purse from his belt.

The artist never remembered how he thanked the priest, or served him the ceremonial tea, or bowed him to his narrow gate. Here at last was a chance for fame and fortune. He felt that this might be all a dream. Why had the Buddha chosen him? He had been too sad to pray often and the housekeeper too busy—could it be that Buddha would listen to the prayers of a little spotted cat? He was afraid that he would wake up and find that the whole thing was an apparition and that the purse was filled with withered leaves. Perhaps he never would have come to himself if he had not been aroused by a very curious noise.

It was a double kind of noise. It was not exactly like any noise that the artist had ever heard. The artist, who was always curious, went into the kitchen to see what could be making the sound, and there, sure enough, were the housekeeper and Good Fortune, and one was crying for joy and one was purring for joy, and it would have been hard to have said which was making more noise. At that the artist had to laugh out loud, but it was not his old sad sort of laugh, this was like a boy's—and he took them both into his arms. Then there were three sounds of joy in the poor old kitchen.

✿   ✿   ✿

One day the artist sat on his mat and his mind wrestled with a more difficult problem than any that had come up before. The gentleness of the snail, the noble strength and wisdom of the elephant, the courage of the horse, the beauty of the wild swan, the willing endurance of the buffalo, the serviceableness of the dog and the generosity of the deer all made it easy to see how they might have served the Buddha, or even have been used by his spirit as temporary dwelling places. So, also, with the wood-pecker, the hare, the goose, the little goat and the ape, all were harmless creatures; and even the lion killed only to appease his hunger and took no joy in the killing.

But the artist knew that the tiger, too, had come to bid farewell to the Buddha, and he, too, had received the master's blessings. How could that be? He thought of the fierceness and cruelty of tigers; he imagined them lying in the striped shadows of the jungle, with their eyes of fire. They were the danger by the water hole, the killers among the reeds. Now and then, one came to the villages and carried away some woman on her way to the well. Or again, one killed a man at work in a field, or carried away a child playing in the dust outside the door of his own house.

What was there in such a creature that the Buddha could bless?

Long and long the artist pondered, sitting in silence, and at last he remembered how devoted a tiger was to his own mate and cubs, and how he would face any odds if these were in danger. He thought, "It may be that this is the narrow pathway by which the tiger reaches to the Buddha. It may be that there is a fierceness in love, and love in fierceness."

So, having opened his mind to the thought of love, even in a tiger, the artist remembered something that he had forgotten until then. Before his mind came a vision of how Siddhartha had won his bride. In open contest with the other princes, he, who was to be the Buddha, had drawn the bow no other hand could draw, had ridden the horse no other man could ride and had shown a skill and strength as a swordsman that none of the others could equal. Watching from her golden palanquin, the princess, Yosadhara sat, her face hidden behind a veil of striped black and gold.

Now at last came the victor's reward. Yosadhara's

father led Siddhartha to his daughter's side, and it was then he whispered, "By your veil I know that you remember how once, in another life, you were a tigress, and I was the tiger who won you in open combat against all the others."

So, among many forms, the Buddha had deigned to take the form of a tiger, as if to prove that even in such a savage life there may be something of greatness. And having once meditated, and now willingly, upon this beautiful creature, sinister but capable of any burning sacrifice, the artist dipped his brush in spring water, touched it with ink, and drew a tiger.

Good Fortune came out from his shadow. When she saw the tiger she trembled all over, from her thistle-down whiskers to her little tail, and looked at the artist.

"If the tiger can come to bid farewell to Buddha," she seemed to say, "surely the cat, who is little and often so gentle, may come, O master? Surely, surely, you will next paint the cat among the animals who were blessed by the Holy One as he died?"

The artist was much distressed.

"Good Fortune," he said, gently taking her into his arms, "I would gladly paint the cat if I could. But all people know that cats, though lovely, are usually proud and self-satisfied. Alone among the animals, the cat refuses to accept the teachings of Buddha. She alone, of all creatures, was not blessed by him. It is perhaps in grief that she, too, often consorts with goblins."

Then Good Fortune laid her little round head against his breast and mewed and mewed like a crying child. He comforted her as well as he could and called for the housekeeper.

"Buy her a fine fish all for herself," he said to the old woman. "And do not let her come here again until the picture is gone. She will break both our hearts."

"Ah, I was afraid she meant to do the painting a harm," said the old woman anxiously. For she felt responsible for having brought the cat home against her master's will, now that their fortunes hung on this painting for the temple.

"It is not that," said the artist, and he returned to his thoughts. How tired, how worn he looked, and yet how beautiful! His picture was almost finished. He had imagined every life. There lay the great figure of the dying Buddha, royal, weary, compassionate. There assembled gods and men; and there were the animals. The scroll of silk seemed scarcely large enough to hold all those varieties of lives, all that gathering of devotion about the welling up of love.

But something was excluded. From the kitchen he heard a faint mewing, and the housekeeper's voice in vain urging Good Fortune to eat. The artist imagined how his little cat felt, so gentle, so sweet, but cursed forever. All the other animals might receive the Buddha's blessing and go to heaven, but the little cat heard the doors of Nirvana closed before her. Tears came to his eyes.

"I cannot be so hardhearted," he said. "If the priests wish to refuse the picture as inaccurate, let them do so. I can starve."

He took up his best brush, dipped it in spring water, touched it with ink, and, last of all the animals, *drew a cat.*

Then he called the housekeeper.

"Let Good Fortune come in," he said. "Perhaps I have ruined us, but I can at least make her happy."

In came Good Fortune, the moment the door was slid open. She ran to the picture, and looked and looked, as though she could never look enough. Then she gazed at the artist with all her gratitude in her eyes. And then Good Fortune fell dead, too happy to live another minute.

The next morning, hearing that the picture was finished, the priest came to see it. After the first greetings, the artist led him in to look at the painting. The priest gazed long.

"How it shines," he said softly.

Then his face hardened.

"But what is that animal whom you have painted last of all?" he asked.

"It is a cat," said the painter, and his heart felt heavy with despair.

"Do you not know," asked the priest sternly, "that the cat rebelled against our Lord Buddha, and did not receive his blessings and cannot enter heaven?"

"Yes, I knew," said the artist.

"Each person must suffer the consequences of his own acts," said the priest. "The cat must suffer from her obstinacy and you from yours. As one can never erase work once done, I will take the painting and tomorrow officially burn it. Some other artist's picture must hang in our temple."

All day the housekeeper wept in the kitchen, for in bringing the little cat home she had, after all, ruined her master.

All day the artist sat in the room beside the hydrangeas and thought. His painting was gone and with it that part of his life which he had put into it. Tomorrow the priests would harshly burn it in the courtyard of the temple. Less than ever would anyone come to him now. He was ruined and all his hopes gone. But he did not regret what he had done. For so many days had he lived in the thought of love and the examples of sacrifice, that it did not seem too hard to suffer for Good Fortune's great moment of happiness.

All night he sat in the darkness open-eyed with his thoughts. The old woman dared not interrupt. He saw the pale light enter through the blinds and heard the dawn wind in the hydrangea bushes. An hour later he heard the noise of people running toward his house. The priests of the temple surrounded him; the head priest pulled at his sleeve.

"Come! Come!" they kept crying. "Come, sir! It is a miracle! Oh, the compassion of Buddha! Oh, the mercy of the Holy One!"

Dazed and breathless, the artist followed them, seeing nothing of the village or the road to the temple. He heard happy voices in his ears, he caught a glimpse of his old housekeeper with her sash askew, and a crowd of open-mouthed neighbors. All together they poured into the temple. There hung the picture with incense and candles burning before it. It was as he had remembered it, but, no!—

The artist sank down on his knees with a cry.

"Oh, the Compassionate One!" For where the last animal had stood was now only white silk that seemed never to have felt the touch of ink; and the great Buddha, the Buddha whom he had painted reclining with hands folded upon his breast, had stretched out an arm in blessing, and under the holy hand knelt the figure of a tiny cat, with pretty white head bowed in happy adoration.

How Cats Came to Purr

by John Bennett

A BOY, having a pet cat which he wished to feed, said to her, "Come, Cat, drink this dish of cream; it will keep your fur as soft as silk, and make you purr like a coffee mill."

He had no sooner said this when the cat, with a great glare of her green eyes, bristled her tail like a gun swab, and went over the back fence, head up first—pop!—as mad as a wet hen.

And this is how she came to do so:

The story is an old one—very, very old. It may be Persian; it may not; that is of very little moment. It is so old that if all the nine lives of all the cats that have ever lived in the world were set up together in a line, the other end of it would just reach back to the time when this occurred.

And this is the story:

Many, many years ago, in a country which was quite

as far from anywhere else as the entire distance thither and back, there was a huge cat that ground coffee in the King's kitchen, and otherwise assisted with the meals.

This cat was, in truth, the actual and very father of all subsequent cats, and his name was Sooty Will, for his hair was as black as night in a coalhole. He was ninety years old, and his mustaches were like whisk brooms. But the most singular thing about him was that in all his life he had never once purred nor humped up his back, although his master often stroked him. The fact was that he never had learned to purr, nor had any reason, so far as he knew, for humping up his back. And being the father of all the cats, there was no one to tell him how. It remained for him to acquire a reason, and from his example to devise a habit which cats have followed from that time forth, and no doubt will forever follow.

The King of the country had long been at war with one of his neighbors; but one morning he sent back a messenger to say that he had beaten his foeman at last, and that he was coming home for an early breakfast as hungry as three bears. "Have batter cakes and coffee," he directed, "hot, and plenty of 'em!"

At that the turnspits capered and yelped with glee, for batter cakes and coffee are not cooked upon spits, and so they were free to sally forth into the city streets and watch the King's homecoming in a grand parade.

But the cat sat down on his tail in the corner and looked cross. "Scat!" said he, with an angry caterwaul. "It is not fair that you should go and that I should not."

"Oh, yes it is," said the gleeful turnspits; "turn and turn about is fair play: you saw the rat that was killed in the parlor."

"Turn about fair play, indeed!" cried the cat. "Then all of you get to your spits; I am sure that is turn about!"

"Nay," said the turnspits, wagging their tails and laughing. "That is over and over again, which is not fair play. 'Tis the coffee mill that is turn and turn about. So turn about to your mill, Sooty Will; we are off to see the King!"

With that they pranced out into the courtyard, turning handsprings, headsprings, and heelsprings as they went, and, after giving three hearty and vociferous cheers in a grand chorus at the bottom of the garden, went capering away for their holiday.

The cat spat at their vanishing heels, sat down on his tail in the chimney corner, and was very glum indeed.

Just then the cook looked in from the pantry. "Hello!" he said gruffly. "Come, hurry up the coffee!" That was the way he always gave his orders.

The black cat's whiskers bristled. He turned to the mill with a fierce frown, his long tail going to and fro like that of a tiger in its lair; for Sooty Will had a temper like hot gunpowder, that was apt to go off sizz, whizz, bang! and no one to save the pieces. Yet, at least while the cook was by, he turned the mill furiously, as if with a right good will.

Meantime, out in the city, a glorious day came on. The sun went buzzing up the pink-and-yellow sky with a sound like that of a walking-doll's works, or of a big

Dutch clock behind a door; banners waved from the castled heights, and bugles sang from every tower; the city gates rang with the cheers of the enthusiastic crowd. Up from cellars, down from lofts, off workbenches, and out of the doors of their masters' shops, dodging the thwacks of their masters' straps, "pop-popping" like corks from the necks of so many bottles, came apprentices, shopboys, knaves, and scullions, crying: "God save the King! Hurrah! Hurrah! Masters and work may go to Rome; our tasks shall wait on our own sweet wills; 'tis holiday when the King comes home. God save the King! Hurrah!"

Then came the procession. There were first three regiments of trumpeters, all blowing different tunes; then fifteen regiments of mounted infantry on coal-black horses, forty squadrons of green and blue dragoons, and a thousand drummers and fifers in scarlet and blue and gold, making a thundering din with their rootle-te-tootle-te-tootle-te-tootle; and pretty well up to the front in the ranks was the King himself, bowing and smiling to the populace, with his hand on his breast; and after him the army, all in shining armor, just enough pounded to be picturesque, miles on miles of splendid men, all bearing the trophies of glorious war, and armed with lances, and bows and arrows, falchions, morgensterns, martels-de-fer, and other choice implements of justifiable homicide, and the reverse, such as hautboys and sackbuts and accordions and Dudelsacks and Scotch bagpipes—a glorious sight!

And, as has been said before, the city gates rang with the cheers of the crowd, crimson banners waved over the city's pinnacled summits, and bugles blew, trumpets brayed, and drums beat until it seemed that wild uproar and rich display had reached their high millennium.

The black cat turned to the coffee mill. "My, oh! My, oh!" he said. "It certainly is not fair that those bench-legged turnspits with feet like so much leather should see the King marching home in his glory, while I, who go shod, as it were, in velvet, should hear only the sound through the scullery windows. It is not fair. It is no doubt true that 'The cat may mew, and the dog shall have his day,' but I have as much right to my day as he;

and has it not been said from immemorial time that 'A cat may look at a King'? Indeed, it has, quite as much as that the dog may have his day. I will not stand for it; it is not fair. A cat may look at a King; and if any cat may look at a King, why, I am the cat who may. There are no other cats in the world; I am the only one. Poh! The cook may shout till his breath gives out, he cannot frighten me, for once I am going to have my fling!"

So he forthwith swallowed the coffee mill, box, handle, drawer knobs, coffee well and all, and was off to see the King.

So far, so good. But, ah! the sad and undeniable truth, that brightest joys too soon must end! Triumphs cannot last forever, even in a land of legends. There comes a reckoning.

When the procession was past and gone, as all processions pass and go, vanishing down the shores of forgetfulness; when barons, marquises, dukes, and dons were gone, with their pennants and banners; when the last lancers had gone prancing past and were lost to sight down the circuitous avenue, Sooty Will, with drooping tail, stood by the palace gate, dejected. He was sour and silent and glum. Indeed, who would not be, with a coffee mill on his conscience? To own up to the entire truth, the cat was feeling decidedly unwell. When suddenly the cook popped his head in at the scullery entry, crying, "How now, how now, you vagabonds! The war is done, but the breakfast is not. Hurry up, scurry up, scamper and trot! The cakes are all cooked and are piping hot! Then why is the coffee so slow?"

The King was in the dining hall, in dressing gown and slippers, irately calling for his breakfast!

The shamefaced, guilty cat ran hastily down the scullery stairs and hid under the refrigerator, with such a deep inward sensation of remorse that he dared not look the kind cook in the face. It now really seemed to him as if everything had gone wrong with the world, especially his own insides. This anyone will readily believe who has ever swallowed a coffee mill. He began to weep copiously.

The cook came into the kitchen. "Where is the coffee?" he said. Then, catching sight of the secluded cat, he stooped, crying, "Where is the coffee?"

The cat sobbed audibly. "Someone must have come into the kitchen while I ran out to look at the King!" he gasped, for there seemed to him no way out of the scrape but by telling a plausible untruth. "Someone must have come into the kitchen and stolen it!" And with that, choking upon the handle of the mill, which projected into his throat, he burst into inarticulate sobs.

The cook, who was, in truth, a very kindhearted man, sought to reassure the poor cat. "There, it is unfortunate, very; but do not weep; thieves thrive in kings' houses!" he said, and, stooping, he began to stroke the drooping cat's back to show that he held the weeping creature blameless.

Sooty Will's heart leaped into his throat.

"Oh, oh!" he half gasped, "Oh, oh! If he rubs his great hands down my back he will feel the corners of the coffee mill through my ribs as sure as fate! Oh, oh! I am a gone cat!" And with that, in an agony of apprehension lest his guilt and his falsehood be thus presently detected, he humped up his back as high in the air as he could, so that the corners of the mill might not make bumps in his sides and that the mill might thus remain undiscovered.

But, alas! he forgot that coffee mills turn. As he humped up his back to cover his guilt, the coffee mill inside rolled over, and, as it rolled, began to grind—*rr-rr-rr-rr-rr-rr-rr-rr-rr-rr!*

"Oh, oh! you have swallowed the mill!" cried the cook.

"No, no," cried the cat, "I was only thinking aloud."

At that out stepped the Genius that Lived under the Great Ovens, and, with his finger pointed at the cat, said in a frightful voice, husky with wood ashes: "Miserable and pusillanimous beast! By telling a falsehood to cover a wrong you have only made bad matters worse. For betraying man's kindness to cover your shame, a curse shall be upon you and all your kind until the end of the world. Whenever men stroke you in kindness, remembrance of your guilt shall make you hump up your back with shame, as you did to avoid being found out. And in order that the reason for this curse shall never be forgotten, whenever man is kind to a cat the sound of the grinding of a coffee mill inside shall perpetually remind him of your guilt and shame!"

With that the Genius vanished in a cloud of smoke.

And it was even as he said. From that day Sooty Will could never abide having his back stroked without humping it up to conceal the mill within him; and never did he hump up his back but the coffee mill began slowly to grind, *rr-rr-rr-rr!* inside him; so that, even in the prime of life, before his declining days had come, being seized upon by a great remorse for these things which might never be amended, he retired to a home for aged and reputable cats, and there, so far as the records reveal, lived the remainder of his days in charity and repentance.

But the curse has come down even to the present day —as the Genius that Lived under the Great Ovens said— and still maintains, though cats have probably forgotten the facts; and so, when stroked, they hump up their backs and purr as if these actions were a matter of pride instead of being a blot upon their family record.

Hey, Diddle, Diddle, the Cat

by Eden Phillpotts

WHEN YOU BE DONE LARNING, you might so well stop living, and for my part, though I'm sixty-five, I thank God as I can still gather useful knowledge when it comes my way.

Fer example, but four years ago, I had my eyes opened about a matter on which I'd thought wrong for more than half a century. I never could understand man or woman who loved a beast; and when I see an old maid dote on her cat, or an old bachelor share the best off his own plate with his dog, I scorned 'em. And when the creatures came to a bad end, as pets so often will, and their owners weren't above shedding a tear for 'em, I said, in my ignorance, they did ought to be ashamed, and called them weak-minded zanies to let a dumb animal reign over 'em in such a fashion. But I don't put on no airs and graces now when I see anybody fretting for a sick or dead creature, because I be in the same boat my-self.

As a widow man and pretty well-to-do, I be one of them that count at Ponsworthy and have always tried to keep up the dignity of the village and be a good neighbor and help on the welfare of us all in my small way. And being addicted to childer, though never blessed or cursed with none, I made friends with the young things and stood well in their opinion.

So it came about that, as I minded their birthdays pretty often, a sharp little maid axed me when mine might be; and I told her, doubting not that she'd forget again. Daisy Bird she was called, the youngest daughter of my particular friend, Martin Bird, of the all-sorts shop.

Well, Daisy remembered, and on my birthday she brought me a kitten just old enough to leave its mother. 'Twas a cat of a well-known mother, but the father was wrapped in mystery, as fathers too often are. The kitling weren't nothing to praise, nor yet to blame—just a very everyday cat, with a piebald face and a bit of yellow and black dabbed about over a white ground. His eyes were doubtful, and Daisy promised me as they'd turn a nice green when he'd growed a bit, same as his mother's; and if you'd look my gift-cat in the mouth, you'd have seen 'twas pink as a rose, with just the beginning of small, pearly teeth coming. No tail to name; but there again Daisy came to the rescue and solemnly vowed that he had the promise of a very fine tail, if I'd only be patient about it.

'Twas to be called "Sunny Jim," and she much hoped

I'd take to it and be a kind friend to it; and if not, it had to be drowned.

I paused at that, for I had meant to beg Daisy to carry it home and let me take the kind will for the deed. But when I see the little thing so trustful and so wishful to please and so well satisfied with me from the first; and when I understood it was a choice between life along with me and death in the river, I hesitated. Daisy picked him up and put him in my hand; and if he'd shown any sauce, or turned against me, it would have been "good-by." But he knew 'twas touch and go and whenever does a cat do a thing that makes against its own prosperity? He looked up in my face and purred, with the little gruff purr as young cats have, and rubbed his small carcass against my waistcoat, as if he'd found the very person he was wanting. So there it stood; I kept him, and let him have his run and his fill, and watched him grow into a very ugly cat in others' eyes—but not ugly to me—never to me.

I always says that it's a beautiful thing to see the contentment of animals. No doubt it only happens because they've got no wits and no power to compare their lot with any other; but whatever it be—horse or donkey, dog or cat, only let him know he's welcome and have got a man or woman friend, and he'll cleave to the lowliest lot and be just so cheerful and good-natured and faithful along with a tinker as a king. They'll fit in, make themselves part of the home, feel 'tis the one place in the world that matters, however poor and humble, and go about the troublesome business of being alive with such pluck and patience and good appetite that they be often a lesson to us grumbling, grizzling humans.

No dog or cat will ever look on the dark side of things. Nature have made 'em hopeful. They be quick to scent pleasure, and though there's good and bad among 'em and some more easily cast down than others, they be prone to welcome life and give of their best in exchange for small mercies.

My Sunny Jim was a very well-named cat. He had what you might call a reasonable mind, and if he'd lacked the many virtues that came out in him, still I'd have been bound in common justice to rate him as a very worthy chap—along of his amazing affection for me. He seemed to know from the first as I had no use for domestic animals, and he said to himself: "Then I'll break you in and make you properly mad about me and conquer your hard heart."

He went about it very cunning, too. He knew I was a terrible clean old man and liked my house to be so spick and span as myself, and so he began by showing me what cleanliness really was; and a more fussy cat from his youth up I have never met. His father must have been a gentleman for sartain. You felt the cat had good blood in him, he was so nice. Never a hair out of place you might say, and he'd lick himself and wash his chops sometimes after a sup and bite till I'd shout at him to let be. Mud was his abomination, and if he come in with a speck on his pads, he'd bite and fidget, as if he was pulling off a pair of gloves; and he never thanked me more grateful nor purred louder than when I gave him his brush and comb. But to tell truth, I humored him in that matter, and finding what a godsend it was to him to have a rub from time to time, I met him there and kept an old brush apurpose.

At six months I knew he'd got me, and I was a lot too fond of the cat; and on his birthday, which Daisy Bird remembered, us gave Sunny Jim a party, and Daisy and half a score of childer agreed to come. 'Twas a great success. Us provided him with three sardines and a drop of cream, and long after the party was over and the childer gone, he sat polishing up. Then, when he felt perfection inside and out, he just gave a sigh of satisfaction and tucked in his paws and sat quite silent thinking over the day's fine doing.

As for mice, he was a very fine performer, but my house never had no mice in it as he soon found, so he went three doors to Mrs. Wilkinson's, where there were scores of dozens, and he never drawed a blank there. Not that he'd often eat a mouse; but he was a mighty hunter of 'em—a proper mouse-tiger, you might say—though not much a one for birds. He seldom went afield and never laid a paw to fur or feathers, like many a hard-bitten poacher of a cat, as makes a shameful end soon or late on gamekeeper's gallows.

He slept along with me, at my bed-foot, and I trained him to come in for his supper an hour or so after dark. But he liked the evening hour and the moth time. Then he'd sit on the party wall and take the air, or join a cat chorus perhaps, but all like a gentleman; and he never went too far or done anything to be ashamed of. A wife or two he may have had, but all well within honor; and he wouldn't fight nor nothing like that, for the good reason that he weighed about five pounds heavier than any cat at Ponsworthy, and no other tom in his right senses would have took him on for a moment.

He supped with me, and by ten o'clock we was both to bed. Then when he was stretched at my feet and the candle out, I'd bid him say his prayers, and he'd purr gentle and steady; and for a good few years the last sound I have heard, as I closed my eyes, was Sunny Jim saying his prayers.

Mrs. Wilkerson warned me, strangely enough, just a week afore the crash came.

"You be putting that tortoise-shell tom afore your God, Peter Blount," she said to me, "and 'tis terrible dangerous, for the Almighty's jealous as the grave, and you may get a nasty awakener."

A proper prophet the woman was, for seven nights later, just afore the hour when the cat was due—a moony night in autumn, bright and peaceful, with the owls calling each other in Western Wood—I heard a harsh, sharp sound which I knowed for a heavy air gun; and not liking it none too well at that late hour, I went in my garden instanter to call Sunny Jim.

The back side of my house gave on waste land that ran up to furze brakes, and I was going to give a look over the wall and see who it might be prowling round, when my cat crawled up to me on three legs. I picked him up and took him in to the lamp; and then I found as he'd got his shoulder all smashed by a bullet.

I kept my head and ministered to the poor soul, and he fixed his eyes upon me and seemed to ask if it was to be a fatal matter. For a time I thought he was sinking, for he lay cruel still with his eyes shut, breathing hard; but then, seeing he weren't in no immediate danger of death, I offered him water, which he lapped, and after that I picked him up so tender as I might, put him in a big vegetable basket, with a bit of blanket in the bottom, and carried him over to Billy Blades.

Bill weren't a man I liked, being a doubtful customer in many ways, and said to have shortened his wife's life by unkindness; but he was a very clever vet and properly renowned for his knowledge of four-footed creatures. He was a great dog fancier without a doubt, and though 'twas whispered he fancied other people's dogs a thought too often, yet the skill was there; so I took Sunny Jim to see the man, and he was home by good luck and gave me all his attention. The cat knew perfectly well what his doctor was up to and behaved like a Christian under the search.

"His shoulder blade be smashed to pieces," said Billy, "and if the ball had took him an inch lower, it would have gone through the creature and slain him. The man who done this made a bad shot, I reckon, and when he found he'd only winged the cat, he ran for it, knowing the creature would have strength to get home and give the show away."

"But why should any mortal man want for to kill my cat?" I asked.

"For his skin," explained Billy Blades. "Cat and coney be worth money nowadays. A skin like this here will dye black and be worth fifteen shillings, or a pound, to any man; and that's why a good few cats have failed to come home lately. But I bain't going to say he won't live. I think he may. He's in good health and in his prime by the look of him, and he's got a patient sort of nature. You see how he bears up. If all goes well and there's no fatal poison in the wound, he'll very likely make a good recovery. Us can't tell yet; but if, as may happen, the wound gets ugly in a few days, then I'll give him a whiff of chloroform and see into the evil and find if the bullet's there."

"I can take hope then?" I asked.

"You can," he said, "but not too much. He's hard hit."

So all was dreadful suspense, and nought could be done for a time till the extent of the danger showed.

I took Sunny Jim home, and, to my great thanksgiving, he ate a bit of raw mutton, as I cut off a leg and minced for him. Not much, but enough to keep up his strength; and he got a little sleep also off and on, though I did not; and in the morning, I carried him down, and he just lay, patient and resigned, on his little mat by the kitchen fire, while I swallowed my breakfast.

But my rage knew no bounds, and if I could have catched the anointed devil as done it, I'd have choked his breath out of him between my hands. I never did feel so properly hard to any fellow creature before; and to this day when I see the vision of thicky cat crawling home on three legs, with the moonlight on his poor, terrified eyes, I feel a thrill of hate and passion.

Next morning it was around the village like a flame of fire that Sunny Jim had been shot and might die of it, and a proper rally of neighbors—women, children, and men—streamed along to see him and say how cruel vexed they was on my account, and to hope that Sunny Jim might be spared. 'Twas the general opinion that no neighbor could have sunk to such a crime, for none was known to bear me a grudge, nor yet him.

Billy Blades came morning and evening to view the patient. And then he gave me a ray of hope, for, in a week, he believed the wound was clean and wouldn't get no worse. In fact, it began to heal very nice outside, and now the danger was whether Sunny Jim's sinews would join up too, or whether they would not. And much depended upon that. He couldn't put his paw down yet, of course, but Job never beat him for patience. He didn't like me out of his sight, however, and wouldn't let down his victuals for anyone but me.

And then in my wrath I issued an advertisement, for I was death on bringing the sinner to justice and felt if a man had done the crime he must be had up and disgraced afore the magistrates; while if it was only a wicked, hardhearted boy, then the least they could do to him, for his own salvation and my satisfaction, would be a darned good hiding.

And I wrote with my own hand six advertisements offering five pounds' reward for the name of the man, or boy, as had shot my famous cat. One I stuck on my front gate, one on the guide post at the crossroads outside Ponsworthy, one in Martin Bird's shopwindow, one in the post office, one by the uppingstock, outside "The Green Man" public house, and the other in the bar of the same.

People marveled at the sight of such big money, and they said, behind my back, as I must be a millionaire, or else going weak in my head; but it was a fortnight afore any response reached me, and then I had the surprise of my life on hearing the sinner's name.

I learnt it of a Friday, when Billy Blades dropped in for a look at Sunny Jim, and he said he was very pleased indeed with the cat's progress, and now felt it was safe to assure me he'd made a recovery and was out of danger.

"The ligaments be joined beautiful," said Billy, "and the bone have growed together. You see how he can use his leg and trust it again; and he could trust it more than he do, only he's nervous yet. But, though he may go a thought lame for life, it will be nothing to interfere with his pleasure. And in time even the lameness may wear away altogether, when the muscles and sinews get used to the change."

Then I thanked Blades with all my heart and shook his hand and told him I thought he was a very clever man and must send in his account.

"And now 'tis all over," he said, "I'll tell you another thing about this cat, and that's the name of the party as tried to shoot him and failed."

"You know!" I cried out. "Then I thank Providence,

Billy; and never shall I part from a five-pound note with better will."

"No, you won't," he answered. "You'll hate to part, Peter; but life's life and cats are cats, and a fiver is a fiver, so just you keep your nerve and take it as it comes. I shot your cat. I was poking about in the furzes with a new air-gun, and seeing the beggar airing himself, I thought a quid for his skin was worth while, me being harder up than usual. So I fired to drop him, but he moved and so was saved alive. Then he was gone like a streak; and so was I, because I knowed you'd fetch him along to me so soon as you could, if he weren't done for. But I'm right down glad to have saved him and be nearly so fond of the chap now as you are yourself."

"You God-forgotten villain!" I cried to the wretch, trembling white with rage.

"I know," he answered. "That's all right, and you can lay it on so thick as you please and cuss till you're winded. But you understand the situation, don't you? You summons me, and I get a dressing down and a caution and a fine. And the fine will be ten shillings and sixpence, and time don't stand still and the matter will soon be forgot; and I get your five pounds."

"Hookem snivey beast!" I said to him. "That ban't all, I promise you! My five pounds you may have; but I'll ruin your business and set every honest man and woman against you, and hound you out of Ponsworthy. By God's light I will!"

He laughed his hateful coarse laugh, and his sharp nose grew sharper than ever.

"You do your worstest and welcome, Peter Blount,"
he said. "I ban't much afraid. There ain't no other vet
within ten miles that I know about, and the farmers don't
care how wicked a man may be, so long as he knows how
to cure their things. So you give me my fiver and then
have me up for trying to shoot your cat. And always remember that I'm terrible glad I missed his vitals—though
how I failed I can't guess, for 'twas bright moonlight and
I was as sober as I am now."

I blazed up at that and ordered him out of my house,
and he went; and I bided awake three parts of the night
thinking on the awful ways of human nature and the
hateful surprises that may be hid in your next-door neigh-

bor and familiar friend. In fact, I cussed Billy and raged against him something furious; and first thing next morning I went up to Martin Bird and catched him taking down his shutters and told him the monstrous tale.

It interested him a lot, and he seemed to think it funny in a way, though for my part I didn't see nothing funny to it.

"To give the traitor as shot Sunny Jim four pounds, ten shilling for his trouble, be a bit of a joke sure enough," said Martin Bird. "Of course, you'll have the satisfaction of getting him up afore the justices and turning public opinion against him; but after all, as he very truly said, a cat's only a cat—masterpiece though your cat is known to be—and the law must hold an even balance between man and man; and when you think of the dark crimes that human nature will do at a pinch, the law have to keep a bit up its sleeve for the murders and such like. And so, no doubt, ten and six for a cat be about the justice of it."

"I don't want no vengeance like that," I told Martin. "We all know vengeance be the Lord's; and to speak plain, I'm a lot more set now on keeping my five-pound note than on having that beastly toad afore the beaks. It ain't the money, but the shame; for he'll have the laugh against me to my dying day if he gets the cash."

"He will," admitted Martin. "Billy Blades is an artful item best of times, and it would hit him much harder to withhold your money than have him up."

"But how can it be done in honesty?" I asked. "There

it is in plain black and white. I offer five pounds to know who shot my cat; and he told me."

Martin Bird said it was a very pretty problem, but he didn't give up all hope of solving it. He was a very clever man, as them with a barrow-load of children must be, if they want to keep their young and themselves out of the workhouse, and he promised me he'd look in during the evening if any light struck upon the subject.

"Anyway, 'tis Saturday, and you can well leave his claim unsettled till you decide whether to summon him," said Bird to me.

So I went home to Sunny Jim and couldn't help feeling that anything less than the law against Billy would be treachery to my cat. And yet again, there was no doubt that Billy had been wondrous clever with the animal, and so healed his shoulder that he was to have the blessing of his leg. For what be the fullness of life to a cat on three legs? Bill had, in fact, made good his own evil work in a manner of speaking, and I was bound to admit that, once the cat was in his hands, he might have finished the murder, and I shouldn't have been none the wiser.

I couldn't see my duty all day, and the more I thought on Billy Blades the more I detested him, for he'd played a devilish part, and not been ashamed to confess it for blood money. So, when Martin strolled in, after he'd shut up his shop, I weren't no forwarder than in the morn. But, if anything I hated worse than ever the thought of handing my five pounds to the assassin.

Martin stroked Sunny Jim for a bit and watched him walk, and said that by the look of it he was making a very brave recovery.

"The bone be joined up and the sinews going on fine," I said to Bird, "and I shall leave him to nature now, for I won't have that cat murderer in my house no more."

"Well," answered Martin, "I believe I see the way out for you. It comes to me, like the Light to Paul, while I was cutting off a pound of bacon. If you want to diddle Billy Bates, it can be done, and you've only got to say the word."

"I do," I said. "I never felt to want nothing so much."

"Right," he answered. "Say no more, Peter, but just go about your business and leave the rest to me."

'Twas a very puzzling direction, and I asked Martin to speak a thought plainer; but he refused.

"See what happens o' Monday morning," was all he would answer. And so, full of wonder and in the dark, I had to leave it at that . . .

Then Bird went his way, but he explained that I needn't grudge it, because he was going to take a tidy bit of trouble on my account. And when he was gone, me and Sunny Jim toddled off to bed. He couldn't quite get upstairs yet, so I had to carry him; and I reckoned that the poor hero had lost about three of his nine lives by this fearful adventure.

Nought happened Sunday, though, as I found afterward, Martin had been as busy as a bee on my account; and when Monday came, afore I'd done my breakfast, and while the cat was washing his face after his, the mystery began to unfold. But when I say "washing his face" I must tell you that Sunny Jim could only polish up one side as yet, for his right front paw couldn't work to perfection so far; and 'twas among his greatest griefs, while he was recovering, that the right side of his head and his right whisker and right ear had to go untended. I done what I could, but nought to satisfy him.

Then who should come in but Andy White, the water-keeper, a very knowledgeable man with the rare gift to see in the dark.

"Well, White," I axed, "and what might you want?"

"Five pounds," he said. "I know who 'twas tried to slay your cat."

I leapt out of my chair as if I was sitting on fire.

"Guy Fawkes and angels!" I cried. "D'you tell me you done it, Andy?"

"Me done it!" he said. "No, Peter Blount, I ban't a cat shooter as ever I heard tell about. And I'm sorry you think I'd so demean myself. 'Twas Neddy Tutt, that young rip from Falcon Farm. He's got an air gun and the deed was his."

Well, for the life of me, I couldn't see even yet what was afoot, and after Andy had said he'd be around with proofs for his money a bit later and had gone to work, I sat marveling at his news.

And then as Mrs. Bassett come in to tidy up for me and see after one thing and another, which she performed regular for half a crown a week, who should knock at the door but Willie Stockman, the shoesmith.

"Hullo, Willie, and what can I do for you?" I asked the

man. He was rather a favorite of mine, for he had a kind heart and kept his widowed mother.

"Ban't what you can do for me, master, but what I can do for you," he answered. "Come in the garden and I'll tell you something you be wishful to know."

So I stepped out, and Sunny Jim, he stepped out with me. You'd have thought the blessed cat was in the know, for he sat and looked at Willie without winking while he spoke.

" 'Tis no less a job than the business of this poor creature," said Stockman. "I happened to be going home in the moonlight with my young woman, and just as us came through the furze brakes up over, I marked a chap with a gun. He lifted it and let fly, and then he was sloking off, and he came full upon us, Peter, and gave us 'Good night.' And 'twas that poaching rascal Timothy Bamsey, from Lower Town. So now you know what you want to know. And I may say your five pounds be going to push on our wedding. There's no hurry, however, till you've got the proofs of the crime."

Of course, I thanked him very gratefully; and when he was gone I beginned slow and sure to see the terrible cunning of Martin Bird. In fact, I'd never have given the man credit for such amazing stratagems; and even that weren't all, for an hour later, as I was digging a few potatoes in the sun, and the cat was practicing his game leg gentle, and seeing if he could clean his claws on the stem of my lilac bush according to his daily use, if Timothy Bamsey himself didn't heave up the road! A hugeous young man—six foot three inches of wickedness, by all accounts. I knew him by sight, no more, and I also knew he'd only escaped clink by the skin of his teeth after a row over the pheasants down to Squire Mannering's preserve. But there he was, and he stopped at the gate and asked in a big voice if I could tell him where I lived.

"Do 'e know the man round about here what had his cat shot long ago?" says Timothy Bamsey to me, and I left my fork sticking in the ground and went down to him.

"I'm the man," I said, "and what about it?" For I felt sure he was come to own the felony and claim the fiver, same as Billy Blades had done. I felt fierce, I admit, for I was getting in a miz-maze along of all this plotting. I'd almost forgot Billy, and for the moment I felt as if I stood face to face with the real, living villain at last.

But he soon undeceived me.

"Well, I know who shot your cat, Master. By chance I was going home along behind these here houses on the right, and just as I came down, I see a man in the moonlight lift a gun and fire—an air gun it was, for there weren't no explosion, but just a whiss and a jolt, like what air guns make. Then he runned forward to take up his prey; but he found nought. He cussed something terrible and was just making off, when he very near ran into me and tried to hide his face. But I see him so plain as I see you this minute."

"And who was the man, Timothy Bamsey?" I asked, as stern as I could.

"Willie Stockman, the shoesmith," he answered. "There ain't no manner of doubt about it, I assure you. And I'll have my fiver, if it's all one, Mr. Blount."

Well, my head was spinning now till I thought it would roll off in the road.

"Us'll talk about this another time," I said to the man. "There's a mystery here, and I must seek friends afore I do ought in such a dark matter. I'm very much obliged to you, and you'll hear of me again presently; but I don't part with no five-pound notes for the minute, for it begins to look as if I should have to summon half the parish afore I get to the bitter truth."

"I've told 'e the truth," he says, "and you owe me five pounds."

"I may, or I may not; but be sure justice shall be done," I said. And with that he went off, leaving me in a proper confusion of brain till the evening come. Then Martin Bird dropped in to hear the result of his work. And when he did hear it he was terrible pleased.

"Now," he said, "you stand firm, for here be a cloud of witnesses, Peter, and one man's word is as good as another's, and better for that matter. Because everybody knows Billy Blades is a liar, and nobody would take his word against t'others'. So all you need to say is that you don't know who to believe among 'em which is true. And then you keep your money in your pocket."

"A masterpiece of politics, Martin!" I said. "And gratefully I thank you for it, but while Sunny Jim's living, it's always in the power of a wicked man to have the last word and lay him out. Don't you forget that."

"I haven't," answered Bird, who fairly staggered me with his wondrous brain power. "I haven't overlooked the future, and what I advise you to do be this, Peter:

ax the whole crew of 'em in to supper one night, and give 'em a tidy feed and a bit of baccy to each. Do 'em a treat; then they'll all be your friends for life."

"And Blades also?" I asked.

"Certainly Blades. He's the one that matters most, 'cause we know he done it in reality. Then, when they be got together and their bellies filled and their pipes drawing suent and their glasses topped up, you can tell 'em, amiable like, that they be a pack of barefaced liars, and you find such a lot of men shot your cat that you ain't going to make any distinctions, but trust to the good will and gentlemanly feeling of 'em all never to do it no more. It will run you in a pound or so, but you're a snug man and won't be none the worse."

"You've took the lead in this matter," I said, "and I'll go through with it according as you direct. All I ask is that you come to the feed with the rest."

Which Martin Bird did do; and, God's my Judge, I never want to spend a pleasanter evening. They all obeyed my invite; and they all laughed fit to die when I told 'em they was a set of low-down, lying blackguards.

Sunny Jim, he much enjoyed his evening, also, and got nothing but kind words. And rabbit pie being very near his favorite food, he done himself so well as any of us. But the merriment tired him, and you can't blame the dear chap for not seeing the joke quite so clear as Billy and Timothy and Martin and Andy and Neddy and Willie saw it.

'Twas a good night, however, and me and Sunny Jim felt very glad to get to bed when the boys had gone.

And this I can say: no hand was ever lifted to my cat again. He walked on his way rejoicing, and though I ban't going to pretend he was ever quite the same light-hearted high-spirited party as of old, yet his higher qualities still shone out of him; and he's all the world to me.

Billy Blades was round only a night ago, and he thought as Sunny Jim ought to live a good five years yet. So I be contented in my mind about him; and while there's a purr left in him, I shall be his very willing servant and faithful friend.

But never again! Life be a cloudy and difficult business enough at best without mixing yourself up with the dumb things and letting a creature without a soul into your heart. I won't love nought on four feet no more. They get too terrible a grip upon your vitals—specially if you're a lonely old blid, without much else to set store by, same as me.

Alice and the Cheshire Cat

by Lewis Carroll

ALICE WAS JUST BEGINNING to think to herself, "Now, what am I to do with this creature when I get it home?" when it grunted again, so violently, that she looked down into its face in some alarm. This time there could be *no* mistake about it: it was neither more nor less than a pig, and she felt that it would be quite absurd for her to carry it any further.

So she set the little creature down, and felt quite relieved to see it trot away quietly into the wood. "If it had grown up," she said to herself, "it would have been a dreadfully ugly child: but it makes rather a handsome pig, I think." And she began thinking over other children she knew, who might do very well as pigs, and was just saying to herself, "If one only knew the right way to change them—" when she was a little startled by seeing the Cheshire Cat sitting on a bough of a tree a few yards off.

The Cat only grinned when it saw Alice. It looked good-natured, she thought: still it had *very* long claws and a great many teeth, so she felt it ought to be treated with respect.

"Cheshire Puss," she began, rather timidly, as she did not at all know whether it would like the name: however, it only grinned a little wider. "Come, it's pleased so far," thought Alice, and she went on, "Would you tell me, please, which way I ought to walk from here?"

"That depends a good deal on where you want to get to," said the Cat.

"I don't much care where—" said Alice.

"Then it doesn't matter which way you walk," said the Cat.

"—so long as I get *somewhere*," Alice added as an explanation.

"Oh, you're sure to do that," said the Cat, "if you only walk long enough."

Alice felt that this could not be denied, so she tried another question. "What sort of people live about here?"

"In *that* direction," the Cat said, waving its right paw round, "lives a Hatter: and in *that* direction," waving the other paw, "lives a March Hare. Visit either you like: they're both mad."

"But I don't want to go among mad people," Alice remarked.

"Oh, you can't help that," said the Cat: "we're all mad here. I'm mad. You're mad."

"How do you know I'm mad?" said Alice.

"You must be," said the Cat, "or you wouldn't have come here."

Alice didn't think that proved it at all; however, she went on: "And how do you know that you're mad?"

"To begin with," said the Cat, "a dog's not mad. You grant that?"

"I suppose so," said Alice.

"Well, then," the Cat went on, "you see a dog growls when it's angry, and wags its tail when it's pleased. Now I growl when I'm pleased, and wag my tail when I'm angry. Therefore I'm mad."

"I call it purring, not growling," said Alice.

"Call it what you like," said the Cat. "Do you play croquet with the Queen today?"

"I should like it very much," said Alice, "but I haven't been invited yet."

"You'll see me there," said the Cat, and vanished.

Alice was not much surprised at this, she was getting so well used to queer things happening. While she was still looking at the place where it had been, it suddenly appeared again.

"By-the-bye, what became of the baby?" said the Cat. "I'd nearly forgotten to ask."

"It turned into a pig," Alice answered very quietly, just as if the Cat had come back in a natural way.

"I thought it would," said the Cat, and vanished again.

Alice waited a little, half expecting to see it again, but it did not appear, and after a minute or two she walked on in the direction in which the March Hare was said to live. "I've seen hatters before," she said to herself: "the

March Hare will be much the most interesting, and perhaps as this is May it won't be raving mad—at least not so mad as it was in March." As she said this, she looked up, and there was the Cat again, sitting on a branch of a tree.

"Did you say pig, or fig?" said the Cat.

"I said pig," replied Alice; "and I wish you wouldn't keep appearing and vanishing so suddenly: you make one quite giddy."

"All right," said the Cat; and this time it vanished quite slowly, beginning with the end of the tail, and ending with the grin, which remained some time after the rest of it had gone.

"Well! I've often seen a cat without a grin," thought Alice; "but a grin without a cat! It's the most curious thing I ever saw in all my life!"

❀   ❀   ❀

The players all played at once without waiting for turns, quarreling all the while, and fighting for the hedgehogs; and in a very short time the Queen was in a furious passion, and went stamping about, and shouting, "Off with his head!" about once in a minute.

Alice began to feel uneasy: to be sure, she had not as yet had any dispute with the Queen, but she knew that it might happen any minute, "and then," thought she, "what would become of me? They're dreadfully fond of beheading people here: the great wonder is, that there's anyone left alive!"

She was looking about for some way of escape, and

wondering whether she could get away without being seen, when she noticed a curious appearance in the air: it puzzled her very much at first, but after watching it a minute or two she made it out to be a grin, and she said to herself, "It's the Cheshire Cat: now I shall have some-body to talk to."

"How are you getting on?" said the Cat, as soon as there was mouth enough for it to speak with.

Alice waited till the eyes appeared, and then nodded. "It's no use speaking to it," she thought, "till its ears have come, or at least one of them." In another minute the whole head appeared, and then Alice put down her fla-mingo, and began an account of the game, feeling very glad she had someone to listen to her. The Cat seemed to think that there was enough of it now in sight, and no more of it appeared.

"I don't think they play at all fairly," Alice began, in rather a complaining tone, "and they all quarrel so dread-fully one can't hear one's self speak—and they don't seem to have any rules in particular; at least, if there are, no-body attends to them—and you've no idea how confusing it is all the things being alive; for instance, there's the arch I've got to go through next walking about at the other end of the ground—and I should have croqueted the Queen's hedgehog just now, only it ran away when it saw mine coming!"

"How do you like the Queen?" said the Cat in a low voice.

"Not at all," said Alice: "she's so extremely—" Just then

she noticed that the Queen was close behind her, listening: so she went on "—likely to win, that it's hardly worth while finishing the game."

The Queen smiled and passed on.

"Who *are* you talking to?" said the King, coming up to Alice, and looking at the Cat's head with great curiosity.

"It's a friend of mine—a Cheshire Cat," said Alice: "allow me to introduce it."

"I don't like the look of it at all," said the King: "however, it may kiss my hand if it likes."

"I'd rather not," the Cat remarked.

"Don't be impertinent," said the King, "and don't look at me like that!" He got behind Alice as he spoke.

"A cat may look at a king," said Alice. "I've read that in some book, but I don't remember where."

"Well, it must be removed," said the King very decidedly, and he called to the Queen, who was passing at the moment, "My dear! I wish you would have this cat removed!"

The Queen had only one way of settling all difficulties, great or small. "Off with his head!" she said without even looking round.

"I'll fetch the executioner myself," said the King eagerly, and he hurried off.

Alice thought she might as well go back and see how the game was going on, as she heard the Queen's voice in the distance, screaming with passion. She had already heard her sentence three of the players to be executed for having missed their turns, and she did not like the look of things at all, as the game was in such confusion that she never knew whether it was her turn or not. So she went off in search of her hedgehog.

The hedgehog was engaged in a fight with another hedgehog, which seemed to Alice an excellent opportunity for croqueting one of them with the other: the only difficulty was, that her flamingo was gone across to the other side of the garden, where Alice could see it trying in a helpless sort of way to fly up into a tree.

By the time she had caught the flamingo and brought it back, the fight was over, and both the hedgehogs were out of sight: "But it doesn't matter much," thought Alice, "as all the arches are gone from this side of the ground."

So she tucked it away under her arm, that it might not escape again, and went back to have a little more conversation with her friend.

When she got back to the Cheshire Cat, she was surprised to find quite a large crowd collected round it: there was a dispute going on between the executioner, the King, and the Queen, who were all talking at once, while all the rest were quite silent, and looked very uncomfortable.

The moment Alice appeared, she was appealed to by all three to settle the question, and they repeated their arguments to her, though, as they all spoke at once, she found it very hard to make out exactly what they said.

The executioner's argument was, that you couldn't cut off a head unless there was a body to cut it off from: that he had never had to do such a thing before, and he wasn't going to begin at his time of life.

The King's argument was, that anything that had a head could be beheaded, and that you weren't to talk nonsense.

The Queen's argument was, that if something wasn't done about it in less than no time, she'd have everybody executed, all round. (It was this last remark that had made the whole party look so grave and anxious.)

Alice could think of nothing else to say but "It belongs to the Duchess: you'd better ask *her* about it."

"She's in prison," the Queen said to the executioner: "fetch her here." And the executioner went off like an arrow.

The Cat's head began fading away the moment he was

gone, and, by the time he had come back with the Duchess, it had entirely disappeared: so the King and the executioner ran wildly up and down looking for it, while the
rest of the party went back to the game.

Benjamin West and His Cat Grimalkin

by Marguerite Henry and Wesley Dennis

BENJAMIN WOKE with a jerk. He held his breath, trying to separate the sounds that came floating up from the inn-yard. Usually he slept through noises. Travelers could lift the latch, help themselves to the snack of food set out for them, warm themselves by the fire, and leave without his so much as hearing them. But tonight there was a small sound that he could not make out.

In a moment everything went quiet. Papa's hound dogs stopped yapping. The rumble of cart wheels died. It was like the stillness that often comes in the middle of a storm.

Benjamin raised himself up on one elbow. He wished he had ears like a horse so that he could swivel around to catch the tiniest sound. There! The little noise came again. It was not the trembling cry of a screech owl. It was not the creaking of the inn signboard, or the frightening howl of a wolf. It sounded more like a boy.

In a flash Benjamin's bare feet were on the stool that acted as a mounting block for his high bed. Soundlessly he dropped to the floor and hurried over to the tiny square window.

He threw open the shutters and poked his head out into the frosty November night.

The courtyard spread out below him, was washed in moonlight. He could see a man leading two scrawny oxen to the shed. He could make out the figures of a woman and a boy on the seat of the oxcart.

Suddenly the boy bent over something in his lap and let out a dry sob.

Benjamin tore off his nightshirt. His clothes lay heaped on a bench in a white patch of moonlight. Quickly he slipped into his leather jerkin and knee breeches. How cold they felt! Perhaps the boy was crying because he was cold. But no, figured Benjamin, as he pulled on his hand-knit stockings and hobnail shoes, it took more than cold to make a boy cry like that.

Shivering, he lifted the latch and tiptoed out into the hall.

"Papa!" he cried, as he collided with Mr. West, who was walking briskly toward him with a candle in his hand. Benjamin tried to straighten the candle which he had tipped at a crazy angle. He daubed at the hot tallow which had spilled down Mr. West's coat.

Then he looked up at his father and, frightened as he

was, he wanted to laugh. In the long shadows made by the candle, his father looked exactly like the scarecrow in Mamma's kitchen garden. The scarecrow wore a sober Quaker jacket and a white nightcap to frighten the crows. And here was Mr. West dressed like the sober Quaker he was, except for a white nightcap perched on his head.

But even with his nightcap on, Papa looked forbidding.

"Benjamin!" he said, his eyebrows scowling. "Must thee meet every guest?"

"No, Papa," replied Benjamin earnestly," but there is a boy crying. A *grown* boy of seven or eight like me."

Papa pulled off his nightcap and tucked it into his pocket. "Come along then," he said. "Step sprightly. I may need thee."

Benjamin followed the black coattails of his father as they flapped down the narrow, winding stairway.

At the foot of the stairs Mr. West lighted the lantern that hung on an iron hook. Then he pinched out his candle and set it on the candle shelf.

Benjamin cast a quick glance around the kitchen. Two Indians lay wrapped in blankets on the floor, their feet to the fire. They grunted in their sleep, then drew their heads into their blankets, like turtles drawing into their shells.

Benjamin and his father singled out their own black hats from the long row that hung on pegs near the door. Then they went out into the night.

In the bright moonlight they saw the boy seated on the upping block used in mounting horses. His parents hovered over him like anxious birds.

"Welcome to Door-Latch Inn in the County of Chester in the Province of Pennsylvania!" spoke Papa in a voice so big it rattled the windows.

The little family started at the sound.

"I am John West, innkeeper," Papa said as he held the lantern high. "And this is my youngest-born, Benjamin."

"So?" said the stranger, shaking hands stiffly. "And I am Johann Ditzler. By me iss my wife and my little feller, Jacob. We come over the seas from the Rhineland. By morning early we make the journey west. Over the mountains we find good land."

Papa nodded. Then he pointed to the boy who sat on the upping block, rocking back and forth, holding something tightly in his arms.

"What," asked Papa, "ails thy boy?"

"Ach," replied Mr. Ditzler, "such troubles we got! Jacob, here, he got a sick kitten. We want he should leave it go, but he cries his eyes out. Tch, tch!"

"Ya," spoke up Mrs. Ditzler. "By Philadelphia it makes down rain. Our big cat and her kitten got all spritzed. Our big cat she dies on us. Soon, now, we lose her kitten. And Jacob iss crying. Chust listen! Such a big boy he iss, too."

Jacob turned to Benjamin for help. In an instant, Benjamin was on his knees, peering into Jacob's arms. And there, lying limp and motionless, was a tiny black kitten. Benjamin listened to its harsh breathing. Then he felt the kitten's nose. "As hot as an ember," he whispered to Jacob.

Benjamin longed to tug at his father's coattails. What kind of way was this to save a sick kitten? Why did grownups waste so much time in talk?

"Animals," Papa was saying, as his breath made little white clouds of steam, "are creatures of God. They need protection in suffering."

The German parents were too tired and cold to do any more talking. All they wanted was a place to lay their heads.

Benjamin could stand the delay no longer.

"Please, Papa!" he whispered. "Elmira, the barn cat, has kittens. Six of them."

He spoke quickly now for fear Papa would not listen to his plan. "She will scarce notice one more."

Papa blinked up at the moon. He frowned. For a long moment he stroked his chin. At last he handed Benjamin the lantern. "Thee may try," he said. "Dr. Moris says a mother cat will oft adopt a hungry kitten. But warm a jug of milk, first. Mayhap the kitten will not need a foster mother."

Benjamin's heart leaped. He suddenly felt as important as Dr. Moris. He could almost feel Dr. Moris' big red bush wig upon his head. But he was glad he was still a boy. He could run!

He ran now across the courtyard, and the barnyard, around the worn path to the cellar. He lifted the heavy trap door and clattered down the coblestone steps, his lantern making long shadows on the wall. He made his

way past barrels of sweet-smelling apples without even stopping to fill his pockets.

The milk crock was full. The good yellow cream had risen to the top. Carefully he ladled it into a tiny jug. Then he hurried into the kitchen. It was bright with fire-light now, and a kettle was singing over the fire.

Mamma was up, pouring hot water into the teapot, spreading rye-an'-Injun bread with rich brown apple butter, saying a quiet word to comfort the little German family, who sat in a row on the hooded settle.

Benjamin glanced at the kitten. It was still breathing. He placed the jug of cream in a little nook in the chimney. "It will soon be warm," he said to Jacob, and smiled a little smile of encouragement. Then he took the rush basket used for gathering eggs and in no time at all he was in the barn, reaching into the haymow for Elmira and one of her kittens.

Elmira struggled, but Benjamin held her and her kitten firmly in the basket. All the while he talked in a soft voice.

"I'll bring thee back to the rest of the family soon," he promised. Then he hurried back to the inn, balancing the basket as carefully as if it held new-laid eggs.

"See!" whispered Benjamin to Jacob as he stroked the big mother cat. "This is Elmira. She will mother thy kitten too. Please put it in the basket."

Gently the boy laid his kitten alongside Elmira's kitten. Then Benjamin set the basket on the floor close to the warmth of the fire.

The room turned quiet. All eyes were on the basket. Not a word was said. Only the fire whistled up the chimney, and the Indians grunted in their sleep.

For two or three seconds the barn cat stared at the strange kitten. Then she sniffed it curiously. Her nose was wrinkled. The fur flew up on her back. Her tail stiffened. "P-h-h-f-t! Sp-f-f-t!" she spat at him. Suddenly, she turned to her own kitten and began washing its face.

Benjamin said a quick prayer under his breath. Please, God, make Elmira be a mother to the sick kitten. Then in case his prayer might not be answered at once he tiptoed around the chimney and reached up for the jug of cream.

"Benjamin!" commanded Mr. West. "Take Elmira back to the barn. Thy plan will not work."

Benjamin was so startled at hearing his father's voice that he upset the jug.

"Oh!" cried Benjamin.

And "Ach!" echoed Jacob as the cream spilled over into the basket, right on top of his kitten.

Now it so happened that Elmira had been raised on skimmed milk. And when she saw the thick yellow cream dripping into the basket, she began licking it from the black kitten's coat.

Up and down went Elmira's head as her pink tongue licked every bit of the rich cream from the kitten's back. And then the strangest thing happened. When all the cream was gone, she kept right on licking. She kept right on stroking the sick kitten with her rough, warm tongue.

Benjamin glanced sidelong at the boy. He laughed out for joy.

Papa clicked his tongue in amazement.

The kitten was stirring ever so slightly. He was stretching! He was letting out a hungry mewing sound.

"Oh!" breathed Benjamin.

"Ach!" sighed Jacob.

Now Elmira was lying on her side, nosing the black kitten and wriggling up to him. After what seemed a long time, but actually was only a matter of seconds, the black kitten began to nuzzle along the barn cat's belly. And at last he and the white kitten were nursing side by side!

A good feeling came over the whole room. Elmira purred until she sounded like a spinning wheel. Then she looked up at the anxious watchers with a pleased smirk on her face.

"Ach, na," clucked Mrs. Ditzler, "everything gets all right!"

"Ai yai yai!" choked Mr. Ditzler as he patted Jacob on the head.

Even Papa seemed happy. He blew his nose as loud as a trumpet.

Why the Cat Stares at the Moon

by M. Grant Cormack

"IF THERE's one animal I hate," said the Cat, "it's Lochag Mouse."

"And what harm did a poor little thing like Lochag ever do to you?" inquired the Dog.

"He pushed me into the river yesterday," said the Cat.

"You mean you were leaning so far over the water to admire your own reflection that you overbalanced and fell in," corrected the Dog. "Lochag was not to blame, however much he laughed. So your first point's not proven. What's the next?"

"He told my mistress that I drank the cream."

"And didn't you?"

"I was just taking the tiniest little sip off the top when Lochag poked his inquisitive head round the meal barrel and squeaked, 'I'll tell!' He must have told, too, for I got beaten for it the very next time I appeared."

"Well, for your information," said the Dog, "Lochag Mouse had nothing to do with that, either. I was lying on the hearthstone when your mistress came in, and the minute she lifted the bowl off the dresser she cried out, 'There are cat's hairs floating in this. Wait till I catch the cat who has stolen my cream!' So there you are—you're not careful enough. It was your own fault."

"And besides," continued the Cat, "it must have been the mouse who told her I knocked the children's vase of marigolds off the window sill and spilt the water on the floor. Nobody else was there to see who had done it— but Lochag would be peeking out from behind his barrel, you might be sure."

"Oh, you talk nonsense!" exclaimed the Dog impatiently. "It wouldn't be hard for her to guess it was you that knocked down the flowers and made such a mess of the place. Sure, whoever goes clambering over the window sills save only yourself? What you do it for I don't know."

"Very well," sniffed the Cat, with her nose in the air, "I can see there's no getting justice from you. I shall just have to deal with Lochag Mouse in my own fashion."

"You watch your step, I warn you!" growled the Dog. "Lochag has plenty of friends to protect him. You'd best leave him alone."

But the Cat turned and spat at him, "P-s-s-st!" Then she ran up the gable end and onto the roof while the Dog scowled at her from below.

From that day began the great battle of wits—Cat versus Mouse. Though the two were evenly matched in speed and cunning, the Cat's superior strength began to tell in her favor. Besides, it is always harder for the pursued than the pursuer—the hunted cannot relax for one moment. Soon the other animals noticed that Lochag was growing thin and haggard. He could never get a bite in comfort, for as soon as the Cat saw his whiskers appear from behind the barrel, she would frighten him back into his hole again. He took to coming out around the hearth at night looking for crumbs when he knew the Cat was shut in the barn; but if by any chance she happened to have been left in the house, then Lochag got nothing to eat till the next night. The Dog took his part, of course, and chased the Cat whenever he could; but as the Dog was often away in the fields working, he could give but little help.

"If I could only have peace to go out at night and do my messages," sighed the little Mouse, "I'd stay in my hole all day without a word of complaint, so I would— but that wicked Cat won't let me!"

It was the Horse who brought up the subject at last. The Horse was interested in Lochag ever since the day the little fellow had taken refuge under his big, hairy hoof; so now he said to the Dog:

"Look here, this Cat-and-Mouse business is a disgrace to the farmyard. Can't you find something to distract the Cat's attention?"

"I've tried," said the Dog, "but the Cat wouldn't pay any heed to me."

"It's time she had her mind fixed on higher things," bleated the Sheep, a pious animal.

"Higher things?" echoed the Dog. "That's an idea!" and he began to chuckle.

The Sheep contemplated him in mild surprise. Dogs! she reflected. Queer animals! There was no use trying to understand them—so she just went on nibbling.

The next night the Dog was lying at the door of his kennel in the moonlight when the Cat came mincing by.

"Hullo, Pussy!" he called.

The Cat stopped short in astonishment. It was a long time since she had had so friendly a greeting addressed to her from that quarter.

"Where are you off to?" asked the Dog.

"Hunting," said she.

"After the Mouse again?" suggested the Dog.

"Maybe I am, maybe I'm not. Do you know where he is?"

"Sure, I know!" answered the Dog.

The Cat came over to him. "Tell me," she pleaded, laying her soft little paw on him. "Please tell me!"

"Can't you guess where he'd be on a lovely night like this? He's gone to visit the Man in the Moon," said the Dog, nodding upward with an expression as solemn as could be.

The Cat's gaze followed his to where the golden globe hung suspended in the heavens. "The—the—Man in the Moon?" she gasped. "How could he get up there?"

"By way of a moonbeam, of course," explained the Dog patiently. "You and I couldn't do it—we're too heavy —but a little thing like Lochag can run along a moonbeam without falling through, and that's where he's gone."

"What did he go all that way for?" asked the Cat. "Just to pay a call?"

The Dog laughed at her ignorance. "Because the moon's made of cheese," he cried. "I thought everyone knew that! You'll see it getting smaller as Lochag nibbles it away; and when there's only a little, thin sliver left he'll come back to earth, till the Man in the Moon makes some more. It's a long way to travel—but wouldn't a Mouse do anything for cheese?"

"I suppose so," admitted the Cat. She was a bit dubious of the story, but she did not venture to contradict the Dog, who had the reputation of being the cleverer ani-

mal. Besides, he was a friend of Lochag's and should know.

"Then, I'll just stay and wait," said the Cat.

"Yes, I'd do that if I were you," the Dog encouraged her. "Keep your eyes on the moon, and you can't miss him."

So saying, he curled up in his kennel and went to sleep, while the Pussycat watched and watched till dawn came and the moon faded right out of the sky.

"Hasn't he arrived yet?" yawned the Dog, stretching himself. "Must have stopped the night. I'd try again to-morrow if I were you. He's sure to come then, unless he decides to stay for the weekend."

So the Cat watched on the second night, and the third, and the fourth. But on the fifth she fell asleep; and that was the night Lochag returned—or so the Dog said. Yet the next time the Cat went in search of the Mouse he was back on the moon. The Dog had seen him go. Lochag's movements became so mysterious and his journeys to and from the moon so frequent that soon the Cat was completely baffled and did not know where he was. And to this day, when she has searched every place she can think of without finding the Mouse, you will notice how the Cat sits and stares at the moon, believing that Lochag is up there eating the cheese. She thinks that if she is only patient and watchful enough, some bright night she will be rewarded by seeing a plump Mouse come sliding down a moonbeam—and she will be there to catch him in her claws. No wonder the Dog laughs!

The Bell and the Cat

from Aesop's Fables

SOME MICE were in great fear of a cat. She watched the place so carefully that not one of them dared venture out from his hole in search of food. They were, therefore, in danger of being starved. In their trouble they called a meeting, and while they were talking the matter over, a conceited young mouse stood up and said:

"Dear friends, after much deep thought I have discovered a plan that will save us all. I propose that we tie a bell round the cat's neck so that by its ringing we shall always know when she is near."

Then he sat down amid great applause. All the mice were delighted with the clever plan, but presently an old mouse, who had not spoken before, said:

"I agree that the plan is excellent, and since our young friend has been so clever as to think of it, perhaps he will tell us also how to carry it out. I want to know who is going to bell the cat?"

Dick Whittington and His Cat

retold by Beth Brown

MANY YEARS AGO, in faraway England, there lived a little lad named Dick Whittington. Both his father and his mother had died while he was still very young. He had no brothers and no sisters, no uncles and no aunts. Dick was alone in the world.

Since he was too young to work and so earn his keep, he had to get along on next to nothing and make the best of it. Now and then, the kindly neighbors, who were just as poor as Dick, gave him a bit of bread or filled a bowl with porridge. The clothes on his back were thin and ragged, and when the harsh wind of winter blew hard, his hands and feet grew cold and white and his cheeks and his nose were red.

But, somehow, summer always rolled around again, and with the warm weather, things seemed a little brighter for Dick. But even in the summertime, he never had enough to eat or a mended coat to wear in order to go to school like other children and learn to read and write.

One day, the loud rumble of a wagon sounded on the dusty road. The horse was strong and happy. The driver was singing a merry song. The man stopped singing when he caught sight of the lad seated under a laurel bush, his blue eyes full of dreams.

"Have you a wish perhaps?" he called down to Dick.

"Yes," answered Dick. "I have three wishes some good fairy could grant."

"What are they?" asked the driver.

"I wish I had enough to eat and clothes on my back and a roof over my head."

"Your wishes are granted!" said the driver. "You will find what you seek—and even more—awaiting you in the great city of London."

"But London," said Dick, "is so far away."

"Hop aboard on the seat beside me," invited the driver, "and I will take you there. As it happens, I am making for Londontown this very day."

Dick came to his feet without waiting an instant and climbed in beside him. Off went the wagon in a cloud of dust and soon the country was far behind him and the blue of adventure lay ahead. As they rode along, the driver talking, his words like a song keeping time with the wheels, told the lad that once he reached London, both food and shelter could easily be had. In fact, the people seldom worked but feasted all day long. The houses were tall and fine. The walks were lined with gold. There was no lack of anything, with plenty of gold for everyone and all the good things that could be had for the clink of a musical gold piece.

"You will see for yourself," the driver said. "We'll be there before the evening."

The countryside was beautiful. The day was fair and warm. At noon, the driver stopped his wagon beside a running stream. He opened his knapsack and took out a chunk of good black bread and a nice big slice of cheese. These he shared with Dick Whittington. He fed and he watered his horse and then they went on their journey.

Dick began singing, too. He rejoiced at his great good fortune. He would soon have food from morning to night, a coat on his back and a strong roof over his head to keep him dry.

Londontown now lay ahead. The driver pulled up his horse and stopped at a curb where he bade the boy farewell.

"Mark my word," he said to Dick. "Here is where you will make your fortune!"

Dick thanked him and watched him go. Then he looked around. To his dismay, he found the streets of London dirty and narrow and steep. The houses were cold and far from handsome. Their faces were grim and uninviting. The crowds were thick and pushed Dick hither and yon. Nobody had a word of greeting for him or gave so much as a smile to the lonely stranger in their midst.

Night fell, cold and damp. Dick sat down on a curbstone. He began to weep bitterly. How he wished he

were back in the country where the friendly song of the
birds filled the air and the sun shone bright of a morning
and the moon beamed kindly at night and the neighbors
called him to come to the door for a bit of bread and
porridge.

A wind came up. The curbstone grew colder and
colder. A coach rumbled past and flung the mud into his
face. Dick shivered and felt chill. He rose unsteadily to
his feet and looked about for a place to sleep. Finally he
found a doorway leading to a fine, white house. He crept
inside in search of shelter, curled himself up in a corner
and tried to catch a wink or two of sleep.

But sleep, it seemed, was out of the question. As it
happened, Dick had picked the home of a wealthy merchant, and the whack of a broom in the hand of one of
the servants soon brought him to his feet.

He ran to the gutter to escape the beating. At that
moment, a coach pulled up and stopped at the door. The
master was arriving home to his fine white house.

"What seems to be the trouble?" he demanded of the
servant.

"A loafer on our doorstep," was the answer. "What's
more, I found him fast asleep."

"Who are you?" asked the merchant, not unkindly.
"What is your name?"

"My name is Dick Whittington," answered the boy. "I
hail from the country a day away."

"What are you doing here in London?"

"I came to make my fortune."

The merchant smiled broadly. "A fortune does not

come so easy, nor does it seek you in sleep. You have to work to make gold."

"I am only too happy to do so. I am willing to work to earn both my board and my keep."

"I am glad to hear you say that," declared the merchant. "There is food and shelter for you under my roof. The cook will put you to work in the kitchen and show you your room for the night."

"Thank you, sir," said Dick. "I will do my very best to please you."

Sure enough he pleased the merchant, and the merchant's daughter as well, and he won warm praise from both. But it was quite another story when it came to pleasing the cook. No matter how hard Dick worked, his only rewards were beatings. Moreover, he was never done with his tasks. Sundays and holidays were no different from other days. Morning, noon and night saw Dick bent over his labors, not only in the kitchen but all through the house.

The dirty pots had to be scrubbed till they were shiny. The dusty floors had to be waxed till they were mirrors. The muddy windows had to be washed till they shone with the glow of diamonds. Dick did his best at all times, and even though his work was good, his daily portion was the wooden end of the broomstick, the leavings of the stew and the stale crusts of the bread.

Now his life was indeed very hard. His garret room afforded little shelter. At night, no sooner did he stumble through the door and stretch himself upon the floor and cover himself for warmth with a few old rags, than the rats and the mice would come out of their holes and swarm all over the attic. Sleep was out of the question. The best he could do was to sit up in a corner with a wooden board for a shield and watch for the dawn to return.

One morning, the merchant gave Dick a coin as a gift for having brushed his coat. That afternoon, while the lad was sweeping the walk outside the house, he saw a little girl come along with a big black cat in her arms.

"How do you do!" greeted Dick Whittington. "My! What a beautiful cat!"

"She is beautiful, isn't she?" said the little girl, stroking the sleek black fur. "Indeed, I wish I could keep her. But we already have a cat at home and my mother says that two cats in a house as small as ours is really one too many. Now what shall I do with Pussy?"

"I will take her from you," said Dick Whittington. "What's more, I will give you my bright coin as a gift."

The little girl was delighted, but not as happy as Dick, because a cat was the very friend he needed to free his attic of rats. However, none of the servants must know about it or both he and his cat would be homeless. So he took off his coat and covered the cat and stole up the steep back stairs high to his garret room.

In the days that followed, Dick shared his food with his new-found friend and in return the cat put an end to the rats and the mice that had filled his nights with horror. And the months flew by and no one troubled to climb to his garret, so his secret was safe and his sleep was sound and a thin smile came to his lips.

One morning, the merchant summoned all his servants to gather in the front parlor. He wore his Sunday coat. His face was grave. His voice was solemn. He had called in his household, he announced, in order to inform them all that he had a ship ready for sailing—and that in return for the loyalty they had shown him and his daughter, he wished to give each one an opportunity to send something aboard in the way of trade.

This sent the servants scuttling back to their rooms.

One brought a mirror. Another brought a lamp. Still another had a bolt of bright red silk. Only Dick had nothing to carry back to the parlor. After all, what did he own in the world? He was only a very poor lad.

"Have you nothing?" said the merchant.

"Nothing," answered Dick.

"Not even so much as a pin?" asked the merchant's daughter.

"Not even so much as a pin," he answered.

"Then I shall give you a jewel box of my own to send along as your own in the way of trade," she offered.

"No, thank you," said Dick, refusing her gift.

The merchant was deep in thought. "Nothing is bad enough," he reflected. "Have you no relatives perhaps?"

"No," answered Dick. "The only thing that is dear to me is my little black cat."

"A cat?" echoed the merchant, and his kind voice matched his smile. "If that is all you have, we will try to trade it for you. Who knows? Everything is good for something. Perhaps someone might even want to buy a

cat. Bring her to me," he told Dick. "We will put her
aboard ship along with all the other wares."

At first, Dick was not inclined to part with his cat. But
the merchant's daughter promised to get him another cat
to take its place and with that, Dick bade farewell to his
friend.

The ship took out to sea.

Meanwhile, at home, the servants piled task upon
task on poor Dick. As if this were not enough to test his
patience, he became the butt of their laughter for having
sent his cat in trade. Who would want a cat, they jeered.
Londontown was full of cats roaming the streets by the
thousands. No doubt there would be cats galore

wherever the good ship anchored and back would come the black cat without so much as a penny piece for Dick.

Their jibes proved too much to bear any longer. So early one morning, Dick washed his face. He combed his hair. He brushed his shoes and started out of London-town on his way back to the country.

This time there was no wagon to give him a lift and the road was hot and dusty. He walked as far as his legs would take him and finally sat down to rest under a welcoming tree that was dripping shade.

While he was resting thus, from far away the bells began to ring. They made a pleasant song for his weary ears. His heart started dreaming again. Yes, why not? Why not fancy himself a fine, rich gentleman of fame and fortune, perhaps the mayor of London? Sure enough, the bells seemed to echo the thread of his thought! They appeared to be ringing out these wonderful words:

"Turn again, Whittington,
Lord Mayor of London!"

Yes, decided Dick. The bells were speaking to him, urging him to return to London in spite of the many tasks in the fine white house and the many beatings he got from the servants. He would work hard, he decided, just as he promised the merchant, and one day, for certain, when he was grown, he would be the Lord Mayor of London.

❖　❖　❖

Meanwhile, the ship, with its holds full of cargo, was battling both sea and storm. The Captain and crew had little time for sleep. They lost both rudder and compass. They found themselves fighting a world of icebergs. Now they were free of the ice. Now the ship drifted. The Captain let it drift off course, hoping the tides would bring it safe into harbor.

Sure enough, the ship bore south. The air grew warm. The coast grew green. And here they were on the coast of Barbary, a strange place among strange people. As the ship rode into port, the natives swam out and swarmed aboard to greet their unexpected guests.

They danced with delight at the fine show of teas and silks and satins with which the ship was loaded. Soon a hundred canoes, filled with good food and fine goods, followed the Captain and crew ashore to the waiting crowds on the sands.

The Court received them royally. The King not only bought all the wares down to the smallest silver thimble as a gift to his lovely Queen but at once he ordered that a feast be spread to honor his royal visitors.

The servants got busy and rolled out the fine big rosy-red carpets, the golden dishes and the silver goblets. The cooks got busy and roasted the meats. The bakers got busy and baked the breads. The gardeners got busy and brought in the fruits.

Now the banquet was ready and the guests were invited to make themselves comfortable and to begin to eat.

But before they were able to take as much as the first

bite of bread, out sprang great swarms of rats and mice. They leaped on the dishes and gobbled up the food. In the twinkling of an eye, all the meat was eaten and the bread was gone.

At this, the servants made haste to run back to the kitchen to bring more meat and bread. But soon, this, too, was eaten by the rats and the mice, without the King or the Queen or the court attendants or the Captain or the crew so much as left the smallest crumb.

The Captain was amazed. He had seen many sights in his travels around the world but nothing to match the march of the rats and the mice upon the royal banquet board.

"And when do you eat?" he asked the King.

"When they are finished!" answered the King in a miserable voice.

"But why not be rid of them?"

"If only I could," replied the King sorrowfully.

"They not only eat our food here in the dining hall," said the weeping Queen, "but take over our bedchamber at night and keep us from sleeping."

"Yes," said the King, "two guards stand on duty beside our bed all through the night for fear we will be attacked."

"Can nothing be done?"

"We have tried everything," replied the King.

"Everything," echoed the Queen.

"I would give half of my kingdom to be rid of the pests. But how?"

"That's easy!" said the Captain. "Just call in your cat. Here is a job that a cat would relish."

"What is a cat?" asked the Queen.

"We have no cat," said the King.

Then they both confessed that they had never heard of such a remarkable creature, much less laid eyes on a cat.

The Captain leaped to his feet. "You will soon see this remarkable creature. I have a cat aboard my ship. I will bring it here to the palace. Soon you will eat in peace. You will sleep like two babes upon your troubled pillows."

"If what you say is true," declared the King, "your reward will indeed be great!" He called to the head cook. "Make ready another banquet for the Captain and his men."

Then the Captain returned with the big black cat in his arms. Again the meat and the bread were ladled out as before and again the rats and the mice swarmed over the food.

But not for long.

The cat leaped into action. Before the startled eyes of the King and his court, the rats and the mice lay dead in great heaps. A few small mice barely managed to escape.

"Don't worry," said the Captain. "These, too, will be destroyed."

Then the third feast was cooked and served, and this time all sat down in peace and in laughter to enjoy the good food the cooks had cooked. Not a mouse showed its nose in the banquet hall.

Night fell.

It was time to leave. The Captain picked up the cat and made ready to take his departure. He thanked the King for his kind hospitality. He gave each of the servants a silver coin as a gift. Then he put a bit of liver in his pocket for the cat and his hat on his head and a smile on his face.

"Farewell," he said. "Farewell."

At this, the Queen began to weep.

The King tried to comfort her. "What is it, my love?"

"The cat—" said the Queen. "Must the Captain take away the cat?"

"I shall ask him," said the King and he turned to the Captain. "I promised you a great store of silver and gold in reward and I am ready to keep my word."

"In that case," said the Captain, smiling broadly, "it's a trade. This remarkable creature is yours." And he placed the cat in the arms of the Queen where the creature soon purred her delight.

*   *   *

The return voyage to England was a merry one. The holds were empty, the money bags full. The weather was fair and the sea was calm and the crew ate all day long and spent the nights singing ditties.

They arrived home hale and hearty.

The Captain was first to take to the gangplank. He carried two great big bags heavy with gold and groaned with great delight under the wonderful weight. The crew walked behind him, each man with a treasure high on his shoulder and a merry whistle on his lips.

They reached the fine, white house of the merchant. Here they set down their silver and their gold. The Captain pounded on the door.

"Open up!" he called. "I come with good news."

"Good morning!" answered the merchant, swinging wide the door. "Good morning indeed!" he echoed when he saw the amount of the treasure.

Soon the Captain and his men were in the parlor and the servants had gathered there, too. All were present but poor, hard-working Dick who was busy in the kitchen scouring the pots and the pans. The merchant sent the cook to fetch him.

"Come at once!" said the cook. "The master has summoned you to the parlor along with the rest of us. The Captain and the crew are here—or did you not know they had come?"

"How can I walk in the parlor dressed in this shabby coat? At least, let me wash my face and my hands and wipe the dust from my shoes."

Soon Dick was ready. He came to the parlor threshold. The merchant stepped up to greet him.

"Come in," he said. "We are waiting for you."

Dick wondered why everyone was smiling so brightly, even the cross-patch cook. To his delight, he soon heard the story of all that had happened since the ship took to sea. Most of the treasure, he learned, that was heaped on the floor, belonged to none other than himself.

But Dick had a heart that was warm and big. He offered the treasure to his master. Of course, the merchant refused. Then Dick declared that unless he could share a part of it with all that were here in the parlor, he would have none of it, not so much as a copper penny.

At this, the merchant relented. He rewarded the Captain and his crew with gifts of gold and of silver and of jewels, while Dick gave a present apiece to each of the servants in the house, including the cook who had beaten him so often and given him so much work.

Needless to say, in the days that followed, Dick came out of the kitchen with its scullery work and soon became a gentleman. He learned to read and to write and to dress in fine clothes. He shared his fortune with the poor of Londontown and in time he married the merchant's daughter and became Lord Mayor of London.

The bells had spoken true. He remained ever humble to the end. He never forgot all that had happened and that he would never have become the great Lord Mayor of London without the help of a cat.

The Cat Who Became Head Forester

by Arthur Ransome

IF YOU drop Vladimir by mistake, you know he always falls on his feet. And if Vladimir tumbles off the roof of the hut, he always falls on his feet. Cats always fall on their feet, on their four paws, and never hurt themselves. And as in tumbling, so it is in life. No cat is ever unfortunate for very long. The worse things look for a cat, the better they are going to be.

Well, once upon a time, not so very long ago, an old peasant had a cat and did not like him. He was a tomcat, always fighting; and he had lost one ear, and was not very pretty to look at. The peasant thought he would get rid of his old cat and buy a new one from a neighbor. He did not care what became of the old tomcat with one ear, so long as he never saw him again. It was no use thinking of killing him, for it is a life's work to kill a cat,

From *Old Peter's Russian Tales* by Arthur Ransome; by permission of Thomas Nelson & Sons Ltd., Edinburgh.

and it's likely enough that the cat would come alive at the end.

So the old peasant took a sack, and he bundled the tomcat into the sack, and he sewed up the sack and slung it over his back, and walked off into the forest. Off he went, trudging along in the summer sunshine, deep into the forest. And when he had gone very many versts into the forest, he took the sack with the cat in it and threw it away among the trees.

"You stay there," says he, "and if you do get out in this desolate place, much good may it do you, old quarrelsome bundle of bones and fur!"

And with that he turned round and trudged home again and bought a nice-looking quiet cat from a neighbor in exchange for a little tobacco, and settled down comfortably at home with the new cat in front of the stove; and here he may be to this day, as far as I know. My story does not bother with him, but only with the old tomcat tied up in the sack away out there in the forest.

The bag flew through the air and plumped down through a bush to the ground. And the old tomcat landed on his feet inside it, very much frightened but not hurt. Thinks he, this bag, this flight through the air, this bump, mean that my life is going to change. Very well, there is nothing like something new now and again.

And presently he began tearing at the bag with his sharp claws. Soon there was a hole he could put a paw through. He went on, tearing and scratching, and there was a hole he could put two paws through. He went on with his work, and soon he could put his head through, all the easier because he had only one ear. A minute or two after that, he had wriggled out of the bag and stood up on his four paws and stretched himself in the forest.

"The world seems to be larger than the village," he said. "I will walk on and see what there is in it."

He washed himself all over, curled his tail proudly up in the air, cocked the only ear he had left, and set off walking under the forest trees.

"I was the head cat in the village," says he to himself. "If all goes well, I shall be head here too." And he walked along as if he were the Tsar himself.

Well, he walked on and on, and he came to an old hut that had belonged to a forester. There was nobody there, nor had there been for many years, and the old tomcat made himself quite at home. He climbed up into the loft under the roof and found a little rotten hay.

"A very good bed," says he, and curls up and falls asleep.

When he woke he felt hungry, so he climbed down and went off in the forest to catch little birds and mice. There were plenty of them in the forest, and when he had eaten enough he came back to the hut, climbed into the loft, and spent the night there very comfortably.

You would have thought he would be content. Not he. He was a cat. He said, "This is a good enough lodging. But I have to catch all of my own food. In the village they fed me every day and I only caught mice for fun. I ought to be able to live like that here. A person of my dignity ought not to have to do all the work for himself."

Next day he went walking in the forest. And as he was walking he met a fox, a vixen, a very pretty young thing, gay and giddy like all girls. And the fox saw the cat and was very much astonished.

"All these years," she said—for though she was young she thought she had lived a long time—"all these years," she said, "I've lived in the forest, but I've never seen a wild beast like that before. What a strange-looking animal! And with only one ear. How handsome!"

And she came up and made her bows to the cat, and said,

"Tell me, great lord, who you are. What fortunate chance has brought you to this forest? And by what name am I to call Your Excellency?"

Oh, the fox was very polite. It is not every day that you meet a handsome stranger walking in the forest.

The cat arched his back and set all his fur on end, and said, very slowly and quietly,

"I have been sent from the far forests of Siberia to be Head Forester over you. And my name is Cat Ivanovitch."

"Oh, Cat Ivanovitch!" says the pretty young fox, and she makes more bows. "I did not know. I beg Your Excellency's pardon. Will Your Excellency honor my humble house by visiting it as a guest?"

"I will," says the cat. "And what do they call you?"

"My name, Your Excellency, is Lisabeta Ivanovna."

"I will come with you, Lisabeta," says the cat.

And they went together to the fox's earth. Very snug, very neat it was inside; and the cat curled himself up in the best place, while Lisabeta Ivanovna, the pretty young fox, made ready a tasty dish of game. And while she was making the meal ready and dusting the furniture with her tail, she looked at the cat. At last she said, shyly,

"Tell me, Cat Ivanovitch, are you married or single?"

"Single," says the cat.

"And I, too, am unmarried," says the pretty young fox, and goes busily on with her dusting and cooking.

Presently she looks at the cat again.

"What if we were to marry, Cat Ivanovitch? I would try to be a good wife to you."

"Very well, Lisabeta," says the cat; "I will marry you."

The fox went to her store and took out all the dainties that she had and made a wedding feast to celebrate her marriage to the great Cat Ivanovitch, who had only one ear, and had come from the far Siberian forests to be Head Forester.

They ate up everything there was in the place.

Next morning the pretty young fox went off busily into the forest to get food for her grand husband. But the old tomcat stayed at home, and cleaned his whiskers and slept. He was a lazy one, was that cat, and proud.

The fox was running through the forest, looking for game, when she met an old friend, the handsome young wolf, and he began making polite speeches to her.

"What had become of you, gossip?" says he. "I've been to all the best earths and not found you at all."

"Let be, fool," says the fox very shortly. "Don't talk to me like that. What are you jesting about? Formerly I was a young, unmarried fox; now I am a wedded wife."

"Whom have you married, Lisabeta Ivanovna?"

"What!" says the fox, "you have not heard that the Cat Ivanovitch, who has only one ear, has been sent from the far Siberian forests to be Head Forester over all of us? Well, I am now the Head Forester's wife."

"No, I had not heard, Lisabeta Ivanovna. And when can I pay my respects to His Excellency?"

"Not now, not now," says the fox. "Cat Ivanovitch will be raging angry with me if I let anyone come near him. Presently he will be taking his food. Look you. Get a sheep and make it ready, and bring it as a greeting to him, to show him that he is welcome and that you know how to treat him with respect. Leave the sheep near by, and hide yourself so that he shall not see you; for, if he did, things might be awkward."

"Thank you, thank you, Lisabeta Ivanovna," says the wolf, and off he goes to look for a sheep.

The pretty young fox went idly on, taking the air, for she knew that the wolf would save her the trouble of looking for food.

Presently she met the bear.

"Good-day to you, Lisabeta Ivanovna," says the bear; "as pretty as ever, I see you are."

"Bandy-legged one," says the fox, "fool, don't come worrying me. Formerly I was a young unmarried fox; now I am a wedded wife."

"I beg your pardon," says the bear, "whom have you married, Lisabeta Ivanovna?"

"The great Cat Ivanovitch has been sent from the far Siberian forests to be Head Forester over us all. And Cat Ivanovitch is now my husband," says the fox.

"Is it forbidden to have a look at His Excellency?"

"It is forbidden," says the fox. "Cat Ivanovitch will be raging angry with me if I let anyone come near him. Presently he will be taking his food. Get along with you quickly; make ready an ox, and bring it by way of welcome to him. The wolf is bringing a sheep. And look you. Leave the ox near by, and hide yourself so that the great Cat Ivanovitch shall not see you; or else, brother, things may be awkward."

The bear shambled off as fast as he could go to get an ox.

The pretty young fox, enjoying the fresh air of the forest, went slowly home to her earth and crept in very quietly, so as not to awaken the great Head Forester, Cat Ivanovitch, who had only one ear and was sleeping in the best place.

Presently the wolf came through the forest, dragging a sheep he had killed. He did not dare to go too near the fox's earth, because of Cat Ivanovitch, the new Head Forester. So he stopped, well out of sight, and stripped off the skin of the sheep, and arranged the sheep so as to seem a nice tasty morsel. Then he stood still, thinking what to do next. He heard a noise, and looked up. There was the bear, struggling along with a dead ox.

"Good-day, brother Michael Ivanovitch," says the wolf.

"Good-day, brother Levon Ivanovitch," says the bear. "Have you seen the fox, Lisabeta Ivanovna, with her husband, the Head Forester?"

"No, brother," says the wolf. "For a long time I have been waiting to see them."

"Go on and call out to them," says the bear.

"No, Michael Ivanovitch," says the wolf, "I will not go. Do you go; you are bigger and bolder than I."

"No, no, Levon Ivanovitch, I will not go. There is no use in risking one's life without need."

Suddenly, as they were talking, a little hare came running by. The bear saw him first and roared out,

"Hi, Squinteye! trot along here."

The hare came up, slowly, two steps at a time, trembling with fright.

"Now then, you squinting rascal," says the bear, "do you know where the fox lives, over there?"

"I know, Michael Ivanovitch."

"Get along there quickly, and tell her that Michael Ivanovitch, the bear, and his brother Levon Ivanovitch, the wolf, have been ready for a long time, and have brought presents of a sheep and an ox, as greetings to His Excellency. . . ."

"His Excellency, mind," says the wolf; "don't forget."

The hare ran off as hard as he could go, glad to have escaped so easily. Meanwhile the wolf and the bear looked about for good places in which to hide.

"It will be best to climb trees," says the bear. "I shall go up to the top of this fir."

"But what am I to do?" says the wolf. "I can't climb a tree for the life of me. Brother Michael, Brother Michael, hide me somewhere or other before you climb up. I beg you, hide me, or I shall certainly be killed."

"Crouch down under these bushes," says the bear, "and I will cover you with the dead leaves."

"May you be rewarded," says the wolf; and he crouched down under the bushes, and the bear covered him up with dead leaves, so that only the tip of his nose could be seen.

Then the bear climbed slowly up into the fir tree, into the very top, and looked out to see if the fox and Cat Ivanovitch were coming.

They were coming; oh, yes, they were coming! The

hare ran up and knocked on the door, and said to the fox,

"Michael Ivanovitch, the bear, and his brother Levon Ivanovitch, the wolf, have been ready for a long time and have brought presents of a sheep and an ox as greetings to His Excellency."

"Get along, Squinteye," says the fox; "we are just coming."

And so the fox and the cat set out together.

The bear, up in the top of the tree, saw them, and called down to the wolf.

"They are coming, Brother Levon; they are coming, the fox and her husband. But what a little one he is, to be sure!"

"Quiet, quiet," whispers the wolf. "He'll hear you, and then we are done for."

The cat came up and arched his back and set his fur on end, and threw himself on the ox, and began tearing the meat with his teeth and claws. And as he tore he purred. And the bear listened and heard the purring of the cat, and it seemed to him that the cat was angrily muttering, "Small, small, small . . ."

And the bear whispers, "He's no giant, but what a glutton! Why, we couldn't get through a quarter of that, and he finds it not enough. Heaven help us if he comes after us!"

The wolf tried to see, but could not, because his head, all but his nose, was covered with the dry leaves. Little by little he moved his head, so as to clear the leaves away from in front of his eyes. Try as he would to be quiet, the leaves rustled ever so little, but enough to be heard by the one ear of the cat.

The cat stopped tearing the meat and listened.

"I haven't caught a mouse today," he thought.

Once more the leaves rustled.

The cat leaped through the air and dropped with all four paws, and his claws cut out, on the nose of the wolf. How the wolf yelped! The leaves flew like dust, and the wolf leaped up and ran off as fast as his legs could carry him.

Well, the wolf was frightened, I can tell you, but he was not so frightened as the cat.

When the great wolf leaped up out of the leaves, the cat screamed and ran up the nearest tree, and that was the tree where Michael Ivanovitch, the bear, was hiding in the topmost branches.

"Oh, he has seen me. Cat Ivanovitch has seen me," thought the bear. He had no time to climb down, and the cat was coming up in long leaps.

The bear trusted to Providence and jumped from the top of the tree. Many were the branches he broke as he fell; many were the bones he broke when he crashed to the ground. He picked himself up and stumbled off, groaning.

The pretty young fox sat still and cried out, "Run, run, Brother Levon! . . . Quicker on your pins, Brother Michael! His Excellency is close behind."

Ever since then, all of the wild beasts have been afraid

of the cat, and the cat and the fox live merrily together and eat fresh meat all the year round, which the other animals kill for them and leave a little way off.

And that is what happened to the old tomcat with one ear, who was sewn up in a bag and thrown away in the forest.

The Cat That Walked by Himself

by Rudyard Kipling

THIS BEFEL and behappened and became and was, O, my Best Beloved, when the tame animals were wild. The Dog was wild, and the Horse was wild, and the Cow was wild, and the Sheep was wild, and the Pig was wild— as wild as could be—and they walked in the wet wild woods by their wild lones, but the wildest of all the wild animals was the Cat. He walked by himself, and all places were alike to him.

Of course the Man was wild too. He was dreadfully wild. He didn't even begin to be tame till he met the Woman and she did not like living in his wild ways. She picked out a nice dry cave, instead of a heap of wet leaves, to lie down in, and she strewed clean sand on the floor, and she lit a nice fire of wood at the back of the cave, and she hung a dried Wild Horse skin, tail down, across the opening of the cave, and she said: "Wipe your feet when you come in, and now we'll keep house."

171

That night, Best Beloved, they ate Wild Sheep roasted on the hot stones and flavored with wild garlic and wild pepper, and Wild Duck stuffed with wild rice, and wild fenugreek and wild coriander, and marrow-bones of Wild Oxen, and wild cherries and wild granadillas. Then the Man went to sleep in front of the fire ever so happy, but the Woman sat up, combing. She took the bone of the shoulder of mutton, the big flat blade-bone and she looked at the wonderful marks on it, and she threw more wood on the fire and she made a magic. She made the first Singing Magic in the world.

Out in the wet wild woods all the wild animals gathered together where they could see the light of the fire a long way off, and they wondered what it meant.

Then Wild Horse stamped with his foot and said: "O, my friends and my enemies, why have the Man and the Woman made that great light in that great cave, and what harm will it do us?"

Wild Dog lifted up his nose and smelled the smell of the roast mutton and said: "I will go up and see and look and stay: for I think it is good. Cat, come with me."

"Nenni," said the Cat. "I am the Cat who walks by himself, and all places are alike to me. I will not come."

"Then we will never be friends again," said Wild Dog, and he trotted off to the cave.

But when he had gone a little way the Cat said to himself: "All places are alike to me. Why should I not go too and see and look and come away?" So he slipped after

Wild Dog softly, very softly, and hid himself where he could hear everything.

When Wild Dog reached the mouth of the cave he lifted up the dried Horse skin with his nose a little bit and sniffed the beautiful smell of the roast mutton, and the Woman heard him and laughed and said: "Here comes the First wild thing out of the wild woods. What do you want?"

Wild Dog said: "O, my enemy and wife of my enemy, what is this that smells so good in the wild woods?"

Then the Woman picked up a roasted mutton bone and threw it to Wild Dog and said: "Wild thing out of the wild woods, taste and try." Wild Dog gnawed the bone and it was more delicious than anything he had ever tasted, and he said: "O, my enemy and wife of my enemy, give me another."

The Woman said: "Wild thing out of the wild woods, help my Man to hunt through the day and guard this cave at night and I will give you as many roast bones as you need."

"Ah!" said the Cat, listening, "this is a very wise Woman, but she is not so wise as I am."

Wild Dog crawled into the cave and laid his head on the Woman's lap and said: "O, my friend and wife of my friend, I will help your Man to hunt through the day, and at night I will guard your cave."

"Ah!" said the Cat, listening, "that is a very foolish Dog." And he went back through the wet wild woods waving his tail and walking by his wild lone. But he never told anybody.

When the Man waked up he said: "What is Wild Dog doing here?" And the Woman said: "His name is not Wild Dog any more, but the First Friend because he will be our friend for always and always and always. Take him with you when you go hunting."

Next night the Woman cut great green armfuls of fresh grass from the water-meadows and dried it before the fire so that it smelt like new-mown hay, and she sat at the mouth of the cave and plaited a halter out of Horse-hide, and she looked at the shoulder of mutton bone—at the big broad blade-bone—and she made a magic. She made the second Singing Magic in the world.

Out in the wild woods all the wild animals wondered what had happened to Wild Dog, and at last Wild Horse stamped with his foot and said: "I will go and see why Wild Dog has not returned. Cat, come with me."

"Nenni," said the Cat. "I am the Cat who walks by himself, and all places are alike to me. I will not come." But all the same he followed Wild Horse softly, very softly, and hid himself where he could hear everything.

When the Woman heard Wild Horse tripping and stumbling on his long mane she laughed and said: "Here comes the Second wild thing out of the wild woods. What do you want?"

Wild Horse said: "O, my enemy and wife of my enemy, where is Wild Dog?"

The Woman laughed and picked up the blade-bone and looked at it and said: "Wild thing out of the wild woods, you did not come here for Wild Dog, but for the sake of this good grass."

And Wild Horse, tripping and stumbling on his long mane, said: "That is true, give it me to eat."

The Woman said: "Wild thing out of the wild woods, bend your wild head and wear what I give you and you shall eat the wonderful grass three times a day."

"Ah," said the Cat, listening, "this is a clever Woman, but she is not so clever as I am."

Wild Horse bent his wild head and the Woman slipped the plaited hide halter over it, and Wild Horse breathed on the woman's feet and said: "O, my mistress and wife of my master, I will be your servant for the sake of the wonderful grass."

"Ah," said the Cat, listening, "that is a very foolish Horse." And he went back through the wet wild woods, waving his wild tail and walking by his wild lone.

When the Man and the Dog came back from hunting the Man said: "What is Wild Horse doing here?" And the Woman said: "His name is not Wild Horse any more, but the First Servant because he will carry us from place to place for always and always and always. Take him with you when you go hunting."

Next day, holding her wild head high that her wild horns should not catch in the wild trees, Wild Cow came up to the cave, and the Cat followed and hid himself just the same as before; and everything happened just the same as before; and the Cat said the same things as before, and when Wild Cow had promised to give her milk to the Woman every day in exchange for the wonderful grass, the Cat went back through the wet wild woods walking by his lone just the same as before.

And when the Man and the Horse and the Dog came home from hunting and asked the same questions, same as before, the Woman said: "Her name is not Wild Cow any more, but the Giver of Good Things. She will give us the warm white milk for always and always and always, and I will take care of her while you three go hunting."

Next day the Cat waited to see if any other wild thing would go up to the cave, but no one moved, so the Cat walked there by himself, and he saw the Woman milking the Cow, and he saw the light of the fire in the cave, and he smelt the smell of the warm white milk.

Cat said: "O, my enemy and wife of my enemy, where did Wild Cow go?"

The Woman laughed and said: "Wild thing out of the wild woods, go back to the woods again for I have braided up my hair and I have put away the blade-bone, and we have no more need of either friends or servants in our cave."

Cat said: "I am not a friend and I am not a servant. I am the Cat who walks by himself and I want to come into your cave."

The Woman said: "Then why did you not come with First Friend on the first night?"

Cat grew very angry and said: "Has Wild Dog told tales of me?"

Then the Woman laughed and said: "You are the Cat who walks by himself and all places are alike to you. You are neither a friend nor a servant. You have said it yourself. Go away and walk by yourself in all places alike."

Then the Cat pretended to be sorry and said: "Must I never come into the cave? Must I never sit by the warm fire? Must I never drink the warm white milk? You are very wise and very beautiful. You should not be cruel even to a Cat."

Then the Woman said: "I knew I was wise but I did not know I was beautiful. So I will make a bargain with you. If ever I say one word in your praise you may come into the cave."

"And if you say two words in my praise?" said the Cat.

"I never shall," said the Woman, "but if I say two words you may sit by the fire in the cave."

"And if you say three words?" said the Cat.

"I never shall," said the Woman, "but if I do you may drink the warm white milk three times a day for always and always and always."

Then the Cat arched his back and said: "Now let the curtain at the mouth of the cave, and the fire at the back of the cave, and the milkpots that stand beside the fire remember what my enemy and the wife of my enemy has said." And he went away through the wet wild woods waving his wild tail and walking by his wild lone.

That night when the Man and the Horse and the Dog came home from hunting, the Woman did not tell them of the bargain that she had made because she was afraid that they might not like it.

Cat went far and far away and hid himself in the wet wild woods by his wild lone for a long time till the Woman forgot all about him. Only the Bat—the little up-side-down Bat—that hung inside the cave knew where Cat hid, and every evening he would fly to Cat with the news.

One evening the Bat said: "There is a Baby in the cave. He is new and pink and fat and small, and the Woman is very fond of him."

"Ah," said the Cat, listening, "but what is the Baby fond of?"

"He is fond of things that are soft and tickle," said the Bat. "He is fond of warm things to hold in his arms when he goes to sleep. He is fond of being played with. He is fond of all those things."

"Ah," said the Cat, "then my time has come."

Next night Cat walked through the wet wild woods and hid very near the cave till morning-time. The woman was very busy cooking, and the Baby cried and inter-rupted; so she carried him outside the cave and gave him a handful of pebbles to play with. But still the Baby cried.

Then the Cat put out his paddy-paw and patted the Baby on the cheek, and it cooed; and the Cat rubbed against its fat knees and tickled it under its fat chin with his tail. And the Baby laughed; and the Woman heard him and smiled.

Then the Bat—the little upside-down Bat—that hung in the mouth of the cave said: "O, my hostess and wife of my host and mother of my host, a wild thing from the wild woods is most beautifully playing with your Baby."

"A blessing on that wild thing whoever he may be," said the Woman straightening her back, "for I was a busy Woman this morning and he has done me a service."

That very minute and second, Best Beloved, the dried Horse-skin curtain that was stretched tail-down at the mouth of the cave fell down—*So!*—because it remembered the bargain, and when the Woman went to pick it up— lo and behold!—the Cat was sitting quite comfy inside the cave.

"O, my enemy and wife of my enemy and mother of my enemy," said the Cat, "it is I, for you have spoken a word in my praise, and now I can sit within the cave for always and always and always. But still I am the Cat who walks by himself and all places are alike to me."

The Woman was very angry and shut her lips tight and took up her spinning-wheel and began to spin.

But the Baby cried because the Cat had gone away, and the Woman could not hush him for he struggled and kicked and grew black in the face.

"O, my enemy and wife of my enemy and mother of my enemy," said the Cat, "take a strand of the thread that you are spinning and tie it to your spindle-wheel and drag it on the floor and I will show you a magic that shall make your Baby laugh as loudly as he is now crying."

"I will do so," said the Woman, "because I am at my wit's end, but I will not thank you for it."

She tied the thread to the little pot spindle-wheel and drew it across the floor and the Cat ran after it and patted it with his paws, and rolled head over heels, and tossed it backward over his shoulder, and chased it between his hindlegs, and pretended to lose it, and pounced down upon it again till the Baby laughed as loudly as he had been crying, and scrambled after the Cat and frolicked all over the cave till he grew tired and settled down to sleep with the Cat in his arms.

"Now," said the Cat, "I will sing the Baby a song that shall keep him asleep for an hour." And he began to purr loud and low, low and loud, till the Baby fell fast asleep. The Woman smiled as she looked down upon the two of them and said: "That was wonderfully done. Surely you are very clever, O, Cat."

That very minute and second, Best Beloved, the smoke of the fire at the back of the cave came down in clouds from the roof because it remembered the bargain, and when it had cleared away—lo and behold!—the Cat was sitting, quite comfy, close to the fire.

"O, my enemy and wife of my enemy and mother of my enemy," said the Cat, "it is I, for you have spoken a second word in my praise, and now I can sit by the warm fire at the back of the cave for always and always and always. But still I am the Cat who walks by himself and all places are alike to me."

Then the Woman was very, very angry and let down her hair and put more wood on the fire and brought out the broad blade-bone of the shoulder of mutton and began to make a magic that should prevent her from saying a third word in praise of the Cat. It was not a Singing Magic, Best Beloved, it was a Still Magic; and by and by the cave grew so still that a little we-wee Mouse crept out of a corner and ran across the floor.

"O, my enemy and wife of my enemy and mother of my enemy," said the Cat, "is that little Mouse part of your magic?"

"No," said the Woman, and she dropped the blade-bone and jumped upon a footstool in front of the fire and braided up her hair very quick for fear that the Mouse should run up it.

"Ah," said the Cat, listening, "then the Mouse will do me no harm if I eat it?"

"No," said the Woman, braiding up her hair; "eat it quick and I will always be grateful to you."

Cat made one jump and caught the little Mouse, and the Woman said: "A hundred thanks to you, O, Cat. Even the First Friend is not quick enough to catch little Mice as you have done. You must be very wise."

That very moment and second, O, Best Beloved, the milkpot that stood by the fire cracked in two pieces—*So!* —because it remembered the bargain, and when the Woman jumped down from the footstool—lo and behold! —the Cat was lapping up the warm white milk that lay in one of the broken pieces.

"O, my enemy and wife of my enemy and mother of my enemy," said the Cat, "it is I, for you have spoken three words in my praise, and now I can drink the warm white milk three times a day for always and always and always. But *still* I am the Cat who walks by himself and all places are alike to me."

Then the Woman laughed and set him a bowl of the warm white milk and said: "O, Cat, you are as clever as a Man, but remember that the bargain was not made with the Man or the Dog, and I do not know what they will do when they come home."

"What is that to me?" said the Cat. "If I have my place by the fire and my milk three times a day I do not care what the Man or the Dog can do."

That evening when the Man and the Dog came into the cave the Woman told them all the story of the bargain, and the Man said: "Yes, but he has not made a bargain with me or with all proper Men after me." And he took off his two leather boots and he took up his little stone axe (that makes three) and he fetched a piece of wood and a hatchet (that is five altogether), and he set them out in a row, and he said: "Now we will make a bargain. If you do not catch Mice when you are in the cave, for always and always and always, I will throw these five things at you whenever I see you, and so shall all proper Men do after me."

"Ah," said the Woman, listening. "This is a very clever Cat, but he is not so clever as my Man."

The Cat counted the five things (and they looked very knobby) and he said: "I will catch Mice when I am in the cave for always and always and always: but still I am the Cat that walks by himself and all places are alike to me."

"Not when I am near," said the Man. "If you had not said that I would have put all these things away (for always and always and always), but now I am going to throw my two boots and my little stone axe (that makes three) at you whenever I meet you, and so shall all proper Men do after me."

Then the Dog said: "Wait a minute. He has not made a bargain with me." And he sat down and growled dreadfully and showed all his teeth and said: "If you are not kind to the Baby while I am in the cave for always and always and always I will chase you till I catch you, and when I catch you I will bite you, and so shall all proper Dogs do after me."

"Ah," said the Woman, listening. "This is a very clever Cat, but he is not so clever as the Dog."

Cat counted the Dog's teeth (and they looked very pointed) and he said: "I will be kind to the Baby while I am in the cave as long as he does not pull my tail too hard for always and always and always. But still I am the Cat that walks by himself and all places are alike to me."

"Not when I am near," said the Dog. "If you had not said that I would have shut my mouth for always and always and always, but now I am going to chase you up a tree whenever I meet you, and so shall all proper Dogs do after me."

Then the Man threw his two boots and his little stone

axe (that makes three) at the Cat, and the Cat ran out
of the cave and the Dog chased him up a tree, and from
that day to this, Best Beloved, three proper Men out of
five will always throw things at a Cat whenever they
meet him, and all proper Dogs will chase him up a tree.
But the Cat keeps his side of the bargain too. He will kill
Mice and he will be kind to Babies when he is in the
house, as long as they do not pull his tail too hard. But
when he has done that, and between times, he is the
Cat that walks by himself and all places are alike to him,
and if you look out at nights you can see him waving his
wild tail and walking by his wild lone—just the same as
before.

The Cat and the Mouse

Traditional

The cat and the mouse
Play'd in the malt-house:

The cat bit the mouse's tail off. "Pray, puss, give me my tail." "No," said the cat, "I'll not give you your tail till you go to the cow and fetch me some milk."

First she leapt, and then she ran,
Till she came to the cow, and thus began:

"Pray, cow, give me milk, that I may give cat milk, that cat may give me my own tail again." "No," said the cow, "I will give you no milk till you go to the farmer and get me some hay."

First she leapt, and then she ran,
Till she came to the farmer, and thus began:

"Pray, farmer, give me hay, that I may give cow hay, that cow may give me milk, that I may give cat milk,

that cat may give me my own tail again." "No," said the
farmer, "I'll give you no hay till you go to the butcher
and fetch me some meat."

First she leapt, and then she ran,
Till she came to the butcher, and thus began:

"Pray, butcher, give me meat, that I may give farmer
meat, that farmer may give me hay, that I may give cow
hay, that cow may give me milk, that I may give cat

milk, that cat may give me my own tail again." "No," said the butcher, "I'll give you no meat till you go to the baker and fetch me some bread."

First she leapt, and then she ran,
Till she came to the baker, and thus began:

"Pray, baker, give me bread, that I may give butcher bread, that butcher may give me meat, that I may give farmer meat, that farmer may give me hay, that I may give cow hay, that cow may give me milk, that I may give cat milk, that cat may give me my own tail again."

"Yes," said the baker, "I'll give you some bread,
But if you eat my meal, I'll cut off your head."

Then the baker gave mouse bread, and mouse gave butcher bread, and butcher gave mouse meat, and mouse gave farmer meat, and farmer gave mouse hay, and mouse gave cow hay, and cow gave mouse milk, and mouse gave cat milk, and cat gave mouse her own tail again.

The White Cat

by Mme. La Comtesse D'Aulnoy
(from the edition arranged by Rachel Field)

ONCE UPON A TIME there was a King who had three sons. The day came when they were grown so big and strong that he began to fear they would be planning to rule in his place. This would cause trouble among themselves and his subjects. Now the King was not so young as he once had been, but, nevertheless, he had no notion of giving up his kingdom then and there. So after much thought he hit upon a scheme which should keep them too busily occupied to interfere in the affairs of state. Accordingly, he called the three into his private apartments where he spoke to them with great kindliness and concern of his plans for their future.

"I am planning to retire from the affairs of state. But I do not wish my subjects to suffer from this change. Therefore, while I am still alive, I shall transfer my crown to one of you. I shall not follow the usual custom of leaving the crown to my eldest son, but whichever one of you shall bring me the handsomest and most intelligent little dog shall become my heir."

The Princes were greatly surprised by this strange request, but they could not very well refuse to humor their father's whim; and since there was luck in it for the two younger sons and the elder of the three was a timid, rather spiritless fellow, they agreed readily enough. The King then bade them farewell after first distributing jewels and money among them and adding that a year from that day at the same place and hour they should return to him with their little dogs.

Within sight of the city gates stood a castle where the three often spent many days in company with their young companions. There they agreed to part and to meet again in a year before proceeding with their trophies to the King; and so having pledged their good faith, and changing their names that they might not be known, each set off upon a different road.

It would take far too long to recount the adventures of all three Princes so I shall tell only of those that befell the youngest, for a more gay and well-mannered Prince never lived, nor one so handsome and accomplished.

Scarcely a day passed that he did not buy a dog or two, greyhounds, mastiffs, bloodhounds, pointers, spaniels, water dogs, lapdogs; but the instant he found a handsomer one he let the first go and kept the new purchase, since it would have been impossible for him to carry them all on his journeyings. He went without fixed plan or purpose, and so he continued for many days, until at last darkness and a terrible storm overtook him at nightfall in a lonely forest. Thunder and lightning rumbled and flashed, rain fell in torrents, the trees seemed to close more densely about him until at last he could no longer find his way. When he had wandered thus for some time, he suddenly saw a glint of light between the tree trunks. Feeling certain that this must mean a shelter of some sort he pressed on till he found himself approaching the most magnificent castle he had ever seen. The gate was of gold and covered with jewels of such brilliance that it was their light which had guided him to the spot. In spite of the rain and storm he caught glimpses of walls of finest porcelain decorated with pictures of the most famous fairies from the beginning of the world up to that very day: Cinderella, Graciosa, Sleeping Beauty, and a hundred others. As he admired all this magnificence he noticed a rabbit's foot fastened to the golden gates by a chain of diamonds. Marveling greatly at such a lavish display of precious gems, the young Prince pulled at the rabbit's foot and straightway an unseen bell of wonderful sweetness rang; the gate was opened by hundreds of tiny hands and others pushed him forward while he hesitated amazed upon the threshold. He moved on wonderingly, his hand on the hilt of his sword until he was reassured by two voices singing a welcome. Again he felt himself being pushed, this time toward a gate of coral opening upon an apartment of mother-of-pearl from which he passed into others still more richly decorated and alight with wax candles and great chandeliers sparkling with a thousand rainbows.

He had passed through perhaps sixty such rooms when the hands that guided him made a sign for him to stop. He saw a large armchair moving by itself toward a fireplace at the same moment that the fire began to blaze and the hands, which he now observed to be very small and white, carefully drew off his wet clothes and handed him others so fine and richly embroidered they seemed fit for a wedding day. The hands continued to dress him, until at last, powdered and attired more handsomely than he had ever been in his life before, the Prince was led into a banquet hall. Here the four walls were decorated solely with paintings, representing famous cats, Puss-in-Boots and others whom he was quick to recognize. Even more astonishing than this was the table set for two with its gold service and crystal cups.

There was an orchestra composed entirely of cats. One held a music book with the strangest notes imaginable, another beat time with a little baton, and all the rest strummed tiny guitars.

While the Prince stared in amazement, each cat suddenly began to mew in a different key and to claw at the guitar strings. It was the strangest music ever heard! The Prince would have thought himself in bedlam had not the palace itself been so marvelously beautiful. So he stopped his ears and laughed heartily at the various poses and grimaces of these strange musicians. He was meditating upon the extraordinary sights he had already seen in the castle, when he beheld a little figure entering the hall. It was scarcely more than two feet in height and wrapped in a long gold crepe veil. Before it walked two cats dressed in deep mourning and wearing cloaks and swords, while still other followed, some carrying rat traps full of rats and mice in cages.

By this time the Prince was too astonished to think. But presently the tiny pink figure approached him and lifted its veil. He now beheld the most beautiful little white cat that ever was or ever will be. She had such a very youthful and melancholy air and a mewing so soft and sweet that it went straight to the young Prince's heart.

"Son of a King," she said to him, "thou art welcome, my mewing Majesty beholds thee with pleasure."

"Madam," responded the Prince, bowing as low as possible before her, "it is very gracious of you to receive me with so much attention, but you do not appear to me to be an ordinary little cat. The gift of speech which you have and this superb castle you inhabit are certainly evidence to the contrary."

"Son of a King," rejoined the White Cat, "I pray that you will cease to pay me compliments. I am plain in my speech and manners, but I have a kind heart. Come," she added, to her attendants, "let them serve supper and bid the concert cease, for the Prince does not understand what they are singing."

"And are they singing words, madam?" he asked incredulously.

"Certainly," she answered, "we have very gifted poets here, as you will see if you remain long enough."

Supper was then served to them by the same hands that

had guided him there, and a very strange meal it was. There were two dishes of each course—one soup, for instance, being of savory pigeons while the other had been made of nicely fattened mice. The sight of this rather took away the Prince's appetite until his hostess, who seemed to guess what was passing in his mind, assured him that his own dishes had been specially prepared and contained no rats and mice of any kind. Her charming manners convinced the Prince that the little Cat had no wish to deceive him, so he began to eat and drink with great enjoyment. During their meal he happened to observe that on one paw she wore a tiny miniature set in a bracelet. This surprised him so that he begged her to let him examine it more closely. He had supposed it would be the picture of Master Puss, but what was his astonishment to find it the portrait of a handsome young man who bore a strange resemblance to himself! As he stared at it, the White Cat was heard to sigh so deeply and with such profound sadness that the Prince became even more curious, but he dared not question one so affected. Instead, he entertained her with tales of court life, with which, to his surprise, he found her well acquainted.

After supper the White Cat led her guest into another hall, where upon a little stage twelve cats and twelve monkeys danced in the most fantastic costumes. So the evening ended in great merriment, and after the Cat had bade the Prince a gracious good night the same strange hands conducted him to his own apartment, where in spite of the softness of his bed he spent half the night trying to solve the mystery of the castle and his extraordinary little hostess.

But when morning came he was no nearer to an answer to his questionings, so he allowed the pair of hands to help him dress and lead him into the palace courtyard. Here a vast company of cats in hunting costume were gathering to the sound of the horn. A fete day indeed! The White Cat was going to hunt and wished the Prince to accompany her. Now the mysterious hands presented him with a wooden horse. He made some objection to mounting it, but it proved to be an excellent charger, and a tireless galloper. The White Cat rode beside him on a monkey, the handsomest and proudest that ever was seen. She had thrown off her long veil and wore a military cap which made her look so bold that she frightened all the mice in the neighborhood. Never was there a more successful hunt. The cats outran all the rabbits and hares, and a thousand skillful feats were performed to the gratification of the entire company. Tiring of the hunt at last, the White Cat took up a horn no bigger than the Prince's little finger and blew upon it with so loud and clear a tone it could be heard ten leagues away. Scarcely had she sounded two or three flourishes when all the cats in the countryside seemed to appear. By land and sea and through the air they all came flocking to her call, dressed in every conceivable costume. So, followed by this extraordinary train, the Prince rode back with his hostess to the castle.

That night the White Cat put on her gold veil again

and they dined together as before. Being very hungry, the Prince ate and drank heartily, and this time the food had a strange effect upon him. All recollection of his father and the little dog he was to find for him slipped from his mind. He no longer thought of anything but of gossiping with the White Cat and enjoying her kind and gracious companionship. So the days passed in pleasant sport and amusement and the nights in feasting and conversation. There was scarcely one in which he did not discover some new charm of the little White Cat. Now he had forgotten even the land of his birth. The hands continued to wait upon him and supply every want till he began to regret that he could not become a cat himself to live forever in such pleasant company.

"Alas," he confessed to the White Cat at last, "how wretched it makes me even to think of leaving you! I have come to love you so dearly. Could you not become a woman or else make me a cat?"

But though she smiled at his wish, the look she turned upon him was very strange.

A year passes away quickly when one has neither pain nor care, when one is merry and in good health. The Prince took no thought of time, but the White Cat was not so forgetful.

"There are only three days left to look for the little dog you were to bring to the King, your father," she reminded him. "Your two brothers have already found several very beautiful ones."

At her words the Prince's memory returned to him and he marveled at his strange forgetfulness.

"What spell would have made me forget what was most important to me in the whole world?" he cried in despair. "My honor and my fortune are lost unless I can find a dog that will win a kingdom for me and a horse swift enough to carry me home again in this short time!"

So, believing this to be impossible, he grew very sorrowful. Then the White Cat spoke to him with great reassurance.

"Son of a King," she said, "do not distress yourself so. I am your friend. Remain here another day, and though it is five hundred leagues from here to your country the good wooden horse will carry you there in less than twelve hours' time."

"But it is not enough for me to return to my father, dear Cat," said the Prince. "I must take him a little dog as well."

"And so you shall," replied she. "Here is a walnut which contains one more beautiful than the Dog Star."

"Your Majesty jests with me," he protested.

"Put the walnut to your ear then," insisted the Cat, "and you will hear it bark."

He obeyed her, and as he held the walnut to his ear a faint "Bow-wow" came from within, more tiny and shrill than a cricket on a winter night. The Prince could scarcely believe his ears or contain his curiosity to see so diminutive a creature. But he was wise enough to follow the White Cat's advice not to open the walnut till he should reach his father's presence.

It was a sad leave-taking between the Prince and the White Cat. A thousand times he thanked her, but though he urged her to return to court with him, she only shook her head and sighed deeply as upon the night of his arrival. So he galloped away at last on the wooden horse, which bore him more swiftly than the wind to the appointed place.

He reached the castle even before his two brothers and enjoyed the sight of their surprise at seeing a wooden horse champing at the bit in the courtyard. The two brothers were so busy telling of their various adventures that they took little note of their younger brother's silence concerning his, but when the time came to show one another their dogs the two were vastly amused at sight of an ugly cur which the young Prince had brought along, pretending to consider it a marvel of beauty. Needless to say the elder Princes smiled with secret satisfaction to think how far superior were their own dogs, for though they wished their brother no ill luck, they had no wish to see him ruling over the kingdom.

Next morning the three set out together in the same coach. The two eldest brothers carried baskets filled with little dogs too delicate and beautiful to be touched, while the youngest carried the poor cur as if it also was precious. By no outward sign did he betray the presence of the walnut with its precious occupant which was safely hidden in his pocket. No sooner did the three set foot in the palace than all the court crowded around to welcome the returned travelers and see the results of their journeyings. The King received them with great joy, professing delight over the little dogs his two elder sons brought out for his inspection. But the more he studied their merits, the more puzzled he became, so nearly were they alike in beauty and grace. The two brothers were already beginning to dispute with one another as to which deserved the crown when the younger brother stepped forward, holding upon the palm of his hand the walnut so lately presented to him by the White Cat. Opening it without more ado, he revealed a tiny dog lying upon cotton. So perfectly formed was it and so small that it could pass through a little finger ring without touching any part of it. It was more delicate than thistledown and its coat shone with colors of the rainbow. Nor was this all, immediately it was released from its kennel, the little creature arose on its hind legs and began to go through the steps of a tarantella, with tiny castanets and all the airs and graces of a Spanish dancer!

The King was dumfounded and even the two brothers were forced to acknowledge that such a beautiful and gifted little dog had never been seen before. But their father was in no mood to give up his kingdom, so he announced that he had decided upon another test of their skill. This time he would give them a year to travel over land and sea in search of a piece of cloth so fine it would pass through the eye of the finest Venetian-point lace needle.

So the Prince remounted his wooden horse and set off at full speed, for now he knew exactly where he wanted to go. So great was his eagerness to see the beautiful White Cat once more that he could scarcely contain himself until her castle came into view. This time every window was alight to welcome him and the faithful pair of hands which had waited on him so well before were ready to take the bridle of the wooden horse and lead it back to the stable while the Prince hurried to the White Cat's private apartments.

He found her lying on a little couch of blue satin with many pillows. Her expression was sad until she caught sight of him. Then she sprang up and began to caper about him delightedly.

"Oh, dear Prince," cried she, "I had scarcely dared to hope for your return. I am generally so unfortunate in matters that concern me."

A thousand times must the grateful Prince caress her and recount his adventures, which perhaps she knew

more about than he guessed. And now he told her of his father's latest whim—how he had set his heart upon having a piece of cloth that could pass through the eye of the finest needle. For his own part he did not believe it was possible to find such a thing, but he believed that if anyone could help him in this quest it would be his dear White Cat. She listened attentively to all he told her and finally explained with a thoughtful air that this was a matter demanding careful consideration. There were, it seemed, some cats in her castle who could spin with extraordinary skill, and she added that she would also put a paw to the work herself so that he need not trouble himself to search farther.

The Prince was only too delighted to accept this offer and he and his charming hostess sat down to supper together, after which a magnificent display of fireworks was set off in his honor. And once more the days passed in enchanted succession. The ingenious White Cat knew a thousand different ways of entertaining her guest, so that he never once thought of missing human society. Indeed, he was probably the first person in the world to spend a whole year of complete contentment with only cats for company.

The second year slipped away as pleasantly as the first. The Prince could scarcely think of anything that the tireless hands did not instantly supply, whether books, jewels, pictures, old things or new. In short, he had but to say, "I want a certain gem that is in the cabinet of the Great Mogul, or the King of Persia, or such and such a statue in Corinth or any part of Greece," and

he saw it instantly before him, without knowing how it
came or who brought it. It is not unpleasant at all to find
oneself able to possess any treasure in the world. No
wonder our Prince was happy!

But the White Cat who was ever watchful of his welfare, warned him that the hour of departure was approaching and that he might make himself easy in his
mind about the piece of cloth, for she had a most wonderful one for him. She added that it was her intention
this time to furnish him with an equipage worthy of his
high birth, and without waiting for his reply, beckoned
him to the window overlooking the castle courtyard.
Here he saw an open coach of gold and flame-color with
a thousand gallant devices to please the mind and eye.
It was drawn by twelve horses as white as snow, four-and-
four abreast, with harnesses of flaming velvet embroidered with diamonds and gold. A hundred other coaches,
each with eight horses and filled with superbly attired
noblemen, followed, escorted by a thousand bodyguards
whose uniforms were so richly embroidered you could
not see the material beneath. But the most remarkable
part of this cavalcade was that a portrait of the White
Cat was to be seen everywhere, in coach device, uni-
form, or worn as a decoration on the doublets of those
who rode in the train, as if it were some newly created
order that had been conferred upon them.

"Go now," said the White Cat to the Prince. "Appear
at the court of the King, your father, in such magnificence that he cannot fail to be impressed and to bestow
upon you the crown which you deserve. Here is another

walnut. Crack it in his presence and you will find the piece of cloth you asked of me."

"Oh, dear White Cat," he answered tenderly, "I am so overcome by your goodness that I would gladly give up my hopes of power and future grandeur to stay here with you the rest of my life."

"Son of a King," she answered, "I am convinced of your kindness of heart. A kind heart is a rare thing among princes who would be loved by all, yet not love anyone themselves. But you are the proof that there is an exception to this rule. I give you credit for the affection you have shown to a little white cat that after all is good for nothing but to catch mice."

So the Prince kissed her paw and departed.

This time the two brothers arrived at their father's palace before him, congratulating themselves that their young brother must be dead or gone for good. They lost no time in displaying the cloths they had brought, which were indeed so fine that they could pass through the eye of a large needle, but not through the small eye of the needle the King had already selected. At this there arose a great murmuring at court. The friends of the two Princes took sides among themselves as to which had fulfilled the bargain better. But this was interrupted by a flourish of trumpets announcing the arrival of their younger brother.

The magnificence of his train fairly took away the breath of the King and his court, but their astonishment grew even greater when, after saluting his father, the young Prince brought out the walnut. This he cracked with great ceremony only to find instead of the promised piece of cloth, a cherry stone. At sight of this the King and the court exchanged sly smiles. Nothing daunted, the Prince cracked the cherry stone, only to find a kernel inside. Jeers and murmurs ran through the great apartment. The Prince must be a fool indeed! He made no answer to them, but even he began to doubt the White Cat's words as he found next a grain of wheat and within that the smallest millet seed. "Oh, White Cat, White Cat! Have you betrayed me?" he muttered between his teeth. Even as he spoke he felt a little scratch upon his hand so sharp that it drew blood. Taking this to be some sort of sign, the Prince proceeded to open the millet seed. Before the incredulous eyes of the whole court he drew out of it a piece of cloth four hundred yards long and marvelously embroidered with colored birds and beasts, with trees and fruits and flowers, with shells and jewels, and even with suns and moons and countless stars. There were also portraits of Kings and Queens of the past upon it and of their children and children's children, not forgetting the smallest child, and each dressed perfectly in the habit of his century.

The sight of this was almost too much for the King. He could scarcely find the needle. Through its eye the wonderful piece of cloth was able to pass not only once but six times, before the jealous gaze of the two older Princes. But the King was still far from ready to give up his kingdom. Once more he turned to his children.

"I am going to put your obedience to a new and final test," he told them. "Go and travel for another year and

whichever one of you brings back with him the most
beautiful Princess shall marry her and be crowned King
on his wedding day. I pledge my honor that after this
I shall ask no further favors of you."

So off the three went again, the youngest Prince still
in a good humor, although he had the least cause to be
since he had twice been the acknowledged winner of
the wager. But he was not one to dispute his father's
will, so soon he and all his train were taking the road
back to his dear White Cat. She knew the very day and
hour of his arrival, and all along the way flowers had
been strewn and perfume made the air sweet. Once
more the castle gate was opened to him and the strange
hands took him in charge while all the cats climbed
into the trees to welcome their returning visitor.

"So, my Prince," said the White Cat when he reached
her side at last, "once more you have returned without
the crown. But no matter," she added as he opened his
lips to explain, "I know that you are bound to take back
the most beautiful Princess to court and I will find one
for you, never fear. Meantime, let us amuse ourselves
and be merry."

The third year passed for the young Prince as had the
two others, and since nothing runs away faster than time
passed without trouble or care, it is certain that he would
have completely forgotten the day of his return to court
had not the White Cat reminded him of it. This time,
however, she told him that upon him alone depended
his fate. He must promise to do whatever she asked of
him. The Prince agreed readily enough until he heard

her command him to cut off her head and tail and fling them into the fire.

"I!" cried the Prince, aghast, "I be so barbarous as to kill my dear White Cat? This is some trick to try my heart, but you should be sure of its gratitude."

"No, no, Son of a King," she answered, "I know your heart too well for that. But fate is stronger than either of us, and you must do as I bid you. It is the only way, and you must believe me, for I swear it on the honor of a Cat."

Tears came into the eyes of the Prince at the mere thought of cutting off the head of so amiable and pretty a creature. He tried to say all the most tender things he could think of, hoping to distract her. But she persisted that she wished to die by his hand because it was the only means of preventing his brothers from winning the crown. So piteously did she beg him that at last, all of a tremble, he drew his sword. With faltering hand he cut off the head and tail of his dear White Cat.

Next moment the most remarkable transformation took place before his very eyes. The body of the little White Cat suddenly changed into that of a young girl, the most graceful ever seen. But this was as nothing compared to the beauty and sweetness of her face, where only the shining brightness of the eyes gave any hint of the cat she had so recently been. The Prince was struck dumb with surprise and delight. He opened his eyes wider still to look at her, and what was his amazement to behold a troop of lords and ladies entering the apartment, each with a cat's skin flung over an arm. They advanced and, throwing themselves at the feet of their Queen, expressed their joy at seeing her once more restored to her natural form. She received them with great affection, but presently she desired them to leave her alone with the Prince.

"Behold, my dear Prince," she said as soon as they had done so, "I am released of a terrible enchantment, too long a tale to tell you now. Suffice it to say that this portrait which you saw upon my paw when I was a cat, was given to me by my guardian fairies during the time of my trial. I supposed it was of my first, unhappy love who was so cruelly taken from me and whose resemblance to you was so striking. Conceive my joy then to find that it is of the Prince who has my entire heart and who was destined to rescue me from my enchantment."

And she bowed low before our Prince, who was so filled with joy and wonder that he would have remained there forever telling her of his love, had she not reminded him that the hour for his return to his father's court was almost upon them. Taking him by the hands, she led him into the courtyard to a chariot even more magnificent than the one she had provided before. The rest were equally gorgeous, the horses shod with emeralds held in place by diamond nails, with such gold and jeweled trappings as were never seen before or since. But the young Prince had eyes for nothing beyond the beauty of his companion.

Just before they reached the outskirts of the city, they sighted the Prince's two brothers with their trains driving toward them from opposite directions. At this the

Princess hid herself in a small throne of rock crystal and precious gems, while the Prince remained alone in the coach. His two brothers, each accompanied by a charming lady, greeted him warmly but expressed surprise and curiosity that he should be alone. To these questions he replied that he had been so unfortunate as not to have met with any lady of sufficient beauty to bring with him to court. He added, however, that he had instead a very rare and gifted White Cat. At this the brothers laughed loudly and exchanged pleased glances, for now they were convinced that he was indeed a simpleton and they need have no fears of his outwitting them a third time.

Through the streets of the city the two elder Princes rode with their ladies in open carriages, while the youngest Prince came last. Behind him was borne the great rock crystal, at which everyone gazed in wonder

The two Princes eagerly charged up the palace stairs with their Princesses, so anxious were they for their father's approval. The King received them graciously, but once more had difficulty in deciding which should have the prize. So he turned to his youngest son, who stood alone before him.

"Have you returned empty-handed this time?" he asked.

"In this rock Your Majesty will find a little White Cat," he answered, "one which mews so sweetly and has such velvet paws that you cannot but be delighted with it."

But before the surprised King could reach the crystal, the Princess touched an inner spring. It flew open revealing her in all her beauty, more dazzling than the sun itself. Her hair fell in golden ringlets; she was crowned with flowers and she moved with incomparable grace in her gown of white and rose-colored gauze. Even the King himself could not resist such loveliness, but hastened to acknowledge her undisputed right to wear the crown.

"But I have not come to deprive Your Majesty of a throne which you fill so admirably," she said, bowing before him graciously. "I was born the heiress to six kingdoms of my own, so permit me to offer one to you and to each of your elder sons. I ask no other favors of you than your friendship and that your youngest son shall be my husband. Three kingdoms will be quite enough for us."

And so in truth they found them.